UNEXPECTED VISITORS

"Hey, there," Joe said cheerfully. "Is Prince Zafir home? We'd like to have a chat with him."

The bodyguard glowered and began closing the door. Joe stuck his foot in the opening. "Not so fast. We'd like to speak to the prince—now."

"It's a business matter," Frank explained quickly. "We work for Mr. Fairfield—"

But before he could get any further, the bodyguard opened the door and stepped outside. Another bodyguard materialized behind him. His eyes were cold and hard.

"Are you getting the feeling that we're not welcome here?" Joe asked Frank uneasily.

Frank didn't have a chance to reply. The first bodyguard said something to the other in Arabic, and the two reached into their pockets. Before Frank knew what was happening, they were brandishing knives—and coming toward him and Joe!

Nancy Drew & Hardy Boys SuperMysteries

Available from ARCHWAY Paperbacks

A NANCY AND HARDY DREW AND BOYS SUPER MYSTERY™

HIGH STAKES

Carolyn Keene

AN ARCHWAY PAPERBACK
Published by POCKET BOOKS
New York London Toronto Sydney Tokyo Singapore

This book is a work of fiction. Names, characters, places and incidents are products of the author's imagination or are used fictitiously. Any resemblance to actual events or locales or persons, living or dead, is entirely coincidental.

AN ARCHWAY PAPERBACK *Original*

An Archway Paperback published by
POCKET BOOKS, a division of Simon & Schuster Inc.
1230 Avenue of the Americas, New York, NY 10020

ISBN: 0-671-53747-4

First Archway Paperback printing November 1996

10 9 8 7 6 5 4 3 2

NANCY DREW, THE HARDY BOYS, AN ARCHWAY
PAPERBACK and colophon are registered trademarks of
Simon & Schuster Inc.

A NANCY DREW AND HARDY BOYS SUPERMYSTERY
is a trademark of Simon & Schuster Inc.

Cover art by Jon Paul

Printed in the U.S.A.

IL 6+

HIGH STAKES

Chapter

One

"I CAN'T BELIEVE we're in Saratoga," George Fayne said, her brown eyes sparkling. "And I can't believe we're having breakfast with a bunch of horses."

Eighteen-year-old Nancy Drew took a sip of her freshly squeezed orange juice and grinned. She and George were at the Saratoga Racetrack in Saratoga Springs, a renowned horse-racing and resort town in upstate New York. They were sitting in an open-air restaurant overlooking the final stretch, where a dozen thoroughbreds were being worked out by their trainers. The same thoroughbreds would be racing that afternoon in front of thousands of spectators.

A roan colt cantered past Nancy and George.

Nancy watched as the colt's trainer, who was dressed in a khaki shirt and pants, a brown riding cap, and leather boots, leaned forward in her saddle and urged him into a gallop.

"He's beautiful, isn't he?" Nancy remarked as the colt took off. "They're *all* beautiful. I can almost understand why people pay so much for them."

"Yeah, but do you *really* know how much they pay?" George tapped her finger on the newspaper that lay next to her coffee cup. "I was reading about a yearling auction that's happening on Saturday. The article said that a yearling named Goldenrod is expected to go for two million dollars, maybe more."

Nancy whistled appreciatively. "Two million dollars. Wow! That seems crazy."

A waitress came by, pad and pencil in hand. "Ready to order, ladies?" she asked.

"We're waiting for two more people," Nancy told her. She glanced at her watch. "It's seven thirty-five. They should be here any minute now."

"No problem," the waitress said.

When she'd left, George leaned across the table. "I can't wait to meet Jimmy. I wonder what he'll be like."

"If he's anything like Eileen," Nancy replied, smiling, "he'll be totally insane and lots of fun."

Nancy and George were in Saratoga on vacation. But they were also in town to see Eileen

Reed, whom they'd met on a camping trip in Vermont. A twenty-one-year-old student at Skidmore College, Eileen was engaged to be married to a guy named Jimmy English. Eileen was bringing Jimmy to breakfast so she could introduce him to Nancy and George.

Just then Nancy spotted Eileen walking into the restaurant. She was just as Nancy remembered her: tiny and waiflike, with a short cap of light brown hair that complemented her small, heart-shaped face. She was wearing a purple plaid sundress over black leggings, and three rhinestone studs in each ear.

Nancy waved to her, and Eileen immediately waved back. "Nancy! George! Hi, guys!" she yelled across the room. People turned to stare at her, but she seemed oblivious.

When Eileen came up to their table, she gave Nancy and George big hugs. "I'm so glad to *see* you!" she gushed. Her hazel eyes swept over the two of them. "You look great!"

"You, too," Nancy told her. "Where's Jimmy?"

Eileen shrugged. "Late as usual. You know newspaper reporters—he's probably chasing down some hot lead and forgotten all about us." She sat down next to George and picked up a menu. "Mmm, blueberry pancakes, eggs Benedict . . ." She giggled. "Remember our breakfasts around the campfire? Burned oatmeal, stale toast, powdered orange juice?"

"Don't remind us," George said, wrinkling her nose.

"It was a terrific idea meeting here," Nancy told Eileen. "It's really fun watching the horses."

As Nancy spoke, several more horses went by. The first one was slender and silvery gray, the second was stocky and dark brown, and the third one was small and black, with a white blaze on its forehead. Their trainers worked them at different speeds: a slow trot, a canter, a full gallop, and then back to a slow trot again.

"Breakfast at the track is one of *the* things to do when you're in Saratoga," Eileen said knowingly.

"So tell us what's going on in your life, Eileen," George said. "How are the wedding plans?"

"Oh, it's all incredibly crazy," Eileen said cheerfully. "We've finally set a date, the Saturday after Thanksgiving, which is only three months away. My parents want us to have the wedding down in Louisiana, but Jimmy and I want to have it here, at this cool old Victorian hotel—"

"The Algonquin?" Nancy asked.

Eileen whacked herself on the forehead. "Oh, yeah. You're staying there, right? Where's my brain? Anyway, they have this ballroom where people can get married. It's total Victorian overload—you know, dark, gloomy furniture, murals with cupids, red velvet drapes, crystal chandeliers. You'll love it."

"Sounds great," George said. "But isn't school starting in a few weeks? How are you going to juggle that with planning the wedding?"

"I have *no* idea," Eileen said with a sigh. "Especially since I'm thinking of changing my major from psych to drama. I'm totally into drama these days. Plus, I just started a job at Lulu's, which puts major stress on my schedule."

"Lulu's?" Nancy asked.

"Lulu's Coffeehouse, on Broadway. You guys have to come down and check it out. Oh, and I'm singing at a club every Monday night. I love it except for the fact that the manager is a total jerk. But what are you going to do, right?" Eileen paused and grinned. "Anyway, my life is a complete madhouse, but I don't care. Jimmy makes me so happy, it's all worth it."

George winked at Nancy. "I think she's in love."

"Definitely," Eileen said. She cast a quick, anxious glance around the room. "I wish he'd get here. I haven't seen him in two days. We were supposed to have dinner last night, but he had to cancel at the last— Oh, there he is. Jimmy! *Jimmy!*"

A very tall, very slender guy was standing in the doorway. He had short blond hair and gold wire-rimmed glasses, and he was dressed in a beige suit. Nancy was struck by the differences between him and Eileen. He was unusually tall, and she was unusually short; he was conservatively dressed, and she was anything but. I guess opposites really do attract, Nancy thought, amused.

Hearing Eileen's voice, Jimmy waved and headed over to the table. When he arrived, Eileen leapt to her feet, threw her arms around his neck, and kissed him on the lips.

Jimmy drew back, blushing slightly. "I'm sorry I'm late," he said, sounding flustered.

Eileen picked up her napkin and wiped lipstick off his mouth. "Where have you been, sweetie?" she asked him merrily. "Working on some big story? Exposing crime and corruption?"

Nancy noticed that Jimmy hesitated a moment before answering. "Um, no," he said. "I just overslept, that's all." He turned to Nancy and George and extended a hand. "You must be Eileen's friends. I'm Jimmy English."

Nancy and George shook his hand and introduced themselves. "So you're a reporter for the local paper," George said. "What's that like?"

"Oh, you know, it's a living," Jimmy replied vaguely. He sat down in the seat across from Eileen, and his gaze wandered to the horses working out on the track. Nancy wondered why he seemed so distracted.

The waitress came by, and Nancy, George, and Eileen ordered.

"And you, hon?" the waitress asked Jimmy.

"Huh? Oh." Jimmy picked up a menu and

glanced at it quickly. "Just a cup of coffee for me."

Eileen touched Jimmy's arm. "Are you okay, sweetie? It's not like you to skip breakfast."

"I'm not very hungry, that's all," Jimmy said.

A shriek erupted across the room. Nancy turned in her seat to see what the commotion was about. A half-dozen girls were flocking around a young guy. He was medium height and lanky, and wore his long, sun-streaked brown hair in a ponytail. He was dressed in jeans and a denim shirt, and his eyes were hidden behind dark glasses.

The guy had a check in hand, and he was clearly trying to leave the restaurant. But the girls stood in his way, holding out papers for his autograph.

"I wonder who he is?" Nancy said.

Eileen peered at him, then gasped. "Oh, wow!" she exclaimed. "I don't believe it! It's Luke Ventura!"

"*The* Luke Ventura?" George said in amazement. "I just saw him in *Love's Revenge.* He was incredible!"

"Plus, he's totally gorgeous," Eileen said, and sighed. Then she quickly put her hand to her lips. "Oops! I'm sorry, Jimmy. I didn't mean that. Of course, you're *much* cuter than Luke Ventura any day."

"Hmm?" Jimmy murmured. "Did you say something?" He glanced across the room. "Oh,

Luke Ventura. He comes to Saratoga every August for the races."

"It seems like *everybody* comes to Saratoga in August for the races," Nancy remarked, tossing her reddish blond hair over her shoulders. "When we got here last night, it was mobbed downtown. Plus, we almost didn't have a place to stay. Our travel agent managed to get the last hotel room in town, and that was only because of a cancellation."

"Well, Saratoga *is* the summer playground of the rich and famous," Eileen told her. "Anyway, if you hadn't scored a hotel room, you could have stayed with me in my tiny little studio apartment. We could have put sleeping bags on the floor and pretended we were camping again." She turned to her fiancé. "Hey, Jimmy, did I tell you how I met Nancy and George?"

As Eileen went on with her story, Nancy noticed that Jimmy was barely listening. He definitely had something on his mind, she thought. But what? And why did Eileen seem oblivious to it?

The waitress appeared with their food. "Belgian waffles, french toast with fresh strawberries, and a Mexican omelette," she recited as she set the plates down. "And a cup of coffee for you, sir," she said to Jimmy.

Jimmy took the cup from her, gulped half of it down, then glanced at his watch. Nancy noticed that it was bright purple, with a cartoon cat on it.

It seemed totally unlike Jimmy. She guessed it was probably a gift from Eileen.

Jimmy pulled some money out of his pocket and set it down on the table. "Breakfast's on me," he announced. "I'm sorry, but I'm going to have to run."

Eileen pouted. "Oh, no! So fast? You just *got* here."

Jimmy leaned across the table and gave her a kiss on the cheek. "Work," he said apologetically. He turned to Nancy and George. "It was really nice meeting you both."

"Thanks for breakfast," George told him.

"Yes, thanks a lot," Nancy added.

Eileen watched Jimmy leave, then she smiled radiantly at Nancy and George. "Isn't he the best?"

"Oh, definitely," Nancy agreed. She paused, then added carefully, "Is he usually so distracted?"

"Oh, I'm sure it's just work stuff," Eileen said, waving dismissively. "Jimmy's really into his job. He wants to be an investigative journalist for one of the big papers someday."

"So he likes getting to the bottom of things." George raised an eyebrow at Nancy. "Just like someone else we know."

"Oh, please," Nancy said with a laugh, then picked up her fork. "The only thing I want to get to the bottom of now are these slices of french toast."

"Now you're talking," Eileen told her. "Come on, guys, eat up! I have a big day of sight-seeing planned for you, and you'll need your energy."

On Thursday morning Nancy woke up to the sound of someone singing. She opened her eyes and ran a hand over the unfamiliar lace bedspread, then stared at the strange wallpaper with the tiny pink roses on it. It took her a second to realize that she was in the Algonquin Hotel and that George was singing in the shower.

Nancy smiled and reached for the alarm clock. It was after nine. "Wow," she said softly to herself. "We really slept in!"

The day before, Eileen had given her and George a whirlwind tour of Saratoga. They'd taken in the beautiful Victorian architecture, a dozen shops, and some great restaurants. Eileen had insisted that they finish their long day by catching her favorite band at one of the clubs, so it had been well past midnight when Nancy and George returned to their hotel room.

Nancy got out of bed, stretched, and wandered over to the window. Pushing aside the gauzy curtain, she gazed out at Broadway, the main street in downtown Saratoga. Across the street were a nineteenth century bank building that had been converted into art studios and a gallery and an old firehouse that was now an Italian restaurant. Although it was only nine o'clock, the sidewalks and outdoor cafés were already jammed, and the mood was festive. Nancy couldn't wait to get outside and explore the town some more.

Just then the phone rang. Nancy walked over and picked it up. "Hello?"

"Nancy? It's me—Eileen." Nancy heard the frantic tone in her friend's voice. "The most terrible thing has happened."

"Eileen, what's going on?"

"Oh, Nancy—" Eileen choked back a sob.

Nancy could tell that her friend was close to hysterics. "Tell me what's wrong."

"Everything's wrong," Eileen wailed. "It's Jimmy. He's disappeared!"

Chapter

Two

NANCY GASPED. "Jimmy's disappeared? When? How?"

"I called him about an hour ago at his apartment, and he wasn't there," Eileen said shakily. "His roommate, Noah, said that he didn't come home last night, which he's never ever done before. That got me worried, so I called the *Saratoga Sentinel* right away."

"That's the paper where he works?" Nancy asked.

"Right," Eileen replied. "His boss said that Jimmy was supposed to be there at seven this morning for an important meeting, but he never showed up. She has no idea where he is, and she's really furious with him." She sniffed and added,

"I know something's wrong! Jimmy would *never* miss a meeting!"

At that moment, George emerged from the bathroom, rubbing her short, curly brown hair with a towel. She raised her brows questioningly at Nancy, and Nancy mouthed the word "Eileen" to her.

Nancy turned her attention back to the phone. "How about Jimmy's car? Did Noah say anything about that?"

"Noah said that it wasn't in the driveway," Eileen told her. "Oh, Nancy, what should I do? Should I call the police?"

Nancy was silent as she considered the situation. "I think we should take this one step at a time," she said slowly. "First of all, I want you to call all the hospitals in the area and make sure Jimmy wasn't admitted last night." Out of the corner of her eye, she saw George's jaw drop.

"The—the hospitals?" Eileen repeated dumbly. "You mean, like, he might have gotten in an accident or something?"

"I'm sure Jimmy's fine," Nancy reassured her. "We just have to cover all the bases. After you're done, come by here and pick us up. I want to go over to Jimmy's apartment. We can look around, and maybe you'll be able to tell if anything is missing—luggage, clothing, stuff like that. Plus, I want to talk to the people at the *Sentinel.*"

"Okay," Eileen agreed. She sniffed again and

added weakly, "Jimmy's okay, isn't he? We're going to find him, aren't we?"

"Of course we will," Nancy told her. But she didn't feel as sure as she sounded. She'd known Jimmy English for only twenty-four hours, but her instincts told her that he was in some sort of trouble.

"This is it," Eileen announced.

She, Nancy, and George were standing in front of a large Victorian house on Caroline Street, a quiet residential street near the downtown area. The house was mauve with plum and green trim. A profusion of summer flowers were in bloom in the front garden: black-eyed Susans, oriental lilies, roses, and gladioli.

Nancy regarded Eileen. Her friend was a wreck. Her eyes were bloodshot from crying, and her face was haggard and pale.

Eileen had shown up at the hotel half an hour earlier. She'd reported to Nancy and George that no one fitting Jimmy's description had been admitted to any of the local hospitals. So the question still remained: Where was he?

"The second floor," Eileen said hollowly. "That's where Jimmy and Noah live, I mean. Their landlord, Mr. Martinez, lives on the first floor."

"Is Noah home now, or is he at work?" Nancy asked.

Eileen gave her a ghost of a smile. "If he's out,

it's not because of a job. Noah's totally allergic to work."

Nancy wondered what Eileen meant by that but decided not to pursue it. Right now she wanted to concentrate on finding Jimmy.

The three of them proceeded to the front door, and Eileen rang the bell. A moment later it was answered by a tall guy in his early twenties. Nancy couldn't believe how handsome he was. His golden blond hair came down to his chin, framing his strong, angular face. He was dressed in gray sweatpants, and he was holding a white T-shirt in his hands. Nancy tried not to stare at his bare, muscular chest.

"Hey, Eileen," he said in a deep voice. His gray eyes surveyed his visitors, lingering on Nancy. "To what do I owe this pleasure?" he added.

"Hi, Noah," Eileen murmured. "These are my friends Nancy Drew and George Fayne. This is Noah Fairfield. We're, um, here about Jimmy."

Noah held the door open wider and bowed. "Do come in. I'm at your service. So, you really think James is missing, huh?"

"We're not sure about anything yet," Nancy answered, glancing quickly at Eileen, who looked dangerously close to crying. "We just want to look through his stuff, see if there might be a clue."

"Nancy's a detective," Eileen explained.

Noah looked interested. "A detective, huh?

Well, come on in. I just made a fresh pot of coffee."

Nancy walked into the apartment, followed by Eileen and George. Nancy was surprised by its luxuriousness. For some reason, she'd expected secondhand furniture, unframed posters tacked to the walls, and dead plants. Instead, the place boasted black leather couches, Art Deco lamps, and large abstract canvases. The voice of the classic jazz singer Billie Holiday emanated from a pair of expensive-looking speakers.

Noah pulled on his T-shirt and disappeared into the kitchen. He emerged minutes later carrying a silver tray. On it were four steaming mugs, a sugar bowl and a cream pitcher, and a plate of scones. "This is decaf French roast, in case anyone's worried about getting too wired," he explained cheerfully.

"This is a nice place," Nancy commented as she sat down on a couch.

Noah set the tray down on the coffee table and gazed at her. Nancy couldn't help but blush. There was something about the way he looked at her that made her feel self-conscious.

"I'm glad you like it, Nancy," he said after a moment. "You were expecting some sort of bachelor pad, right? Empty pizza boxes, clothes on the floor, bookshelves made out of milk crates?"

"N-no," Nancy stammered. How did he know? she wondered.

Eileen and George sat down on the couch on either side of Nancy. They all took a mug of coffee.

Nancy tried to compose her thoughts. She wanted to ask Noah some questions about Jimmy. "So, Noah, when was the last time you saw Jimmy?"

Noah sat down on the couch across from them and steepled his hands under his chin. "Let's see," he repeated slowly. "Yesterday morning, before he took off to have breakfast with you all."

"Do you know if he came back to the apartment anytime after that?" George asked him.

"I was out yesterday from noon to five, so I can't tell you about then," Noah replied. "But I was here the rest of the time. Jimmy never showed up."

Nancy took a sip of her coffee. It was strong and delicious. "How did he seem to you yesterday morning?"

Noah shrugged. "I saw him for all of five minutes, so it's hard to say. He did seem a little preoccupied. He forgot his car keys and had to come back for them."

Nancy was silent. Then she had a thought. "How about Jimmy's relatives? Is it possible there was a family emergency and he took off without telling anyone?"

Eileen shook her head. "Jimmy's parents are in Europe right now—they're celebrating their twenty-fifth wedding anniversary. And he doesn't have any brothers or sisters."

"How about close friends?" George suggested.

Noah turned to Eileen. "Why don't I try calling Josh and Raj? And maybe Seito, too? It's possible that one of them has heard from him."

"That would be great, Noah," Eileen said gratefully. "While you're at it, try Hal."

"You got it." Noah picked up the cordless phone from the coffee table and began punching numbers. "Hello?" he said after a moment. "Josh? Hey, man, it's Noah. Listen, I was wondering if you've spoken to Jimmy E. in the last few days. . . ."

While Noah was busy making calls, Nancy, Eileen, and George decided to check out Jimmy's room. It was large and sunny, with a double bed, dresser, and desk. On top of the desk were some magazines, a pile of papers, and a framed photograph of Jimmy and Eileen. He had his arm around her, and they were smiling.

Nancy sat down at the desk and began looking through the pile of papers. "Do you know if Jimmy has an appointment calendar?" she asked Eileen.

"Definitely," Eileen replied. "I think he usually carries it with him, though."

George sat down on the edge of the bed. "So the last time you talked to him was at breakfast yesterday, huh? Do you know what his plans were for the rest of the day and night?"

"Well, I know he was going to work after he left us," Eileen said slowly. "But as for last night—I don't know."

Nancy found nothing of interest in Jimmy's papers. They consisted mostly of bills, personal correspondence, and to-do lists. Nancy observed that Jimmy's handwriting was scratchy and that he often abbreviated words in the style typical of journalists. There was no appointment calendar or anything else indicating his schedule.

"Let's try his dresser and closet next," Nancy said, rising to her feet. "I want to check for anything that might point to a trip."

But after searching for several minutes, the girls came up empty-handed. "It looks like all his clothes are here, except for the suit he was wearing yesterday," Eileen noted. She pointed to a brown leather overnight bag that was sitting in the closet. "Plus, he always takes that bag on trips. And since it's here . . ." Her words trailed off.

The door opened, and Noah walked into the room. He glanced briefly at Nancy, who was still going through Jimmy's closet, then fixed his eyes on Eileen. "No one's heard from Jimmy," he announced, "and no one knows where he might have gone."

"Oh, great," Eileen said dejectedly.

"Hey, what's this?" Nancy said suddenly. Tucked into the pocket of one of Jimmy's blazers was a newspaper clipping. Nancy pulled it out and scanned it quickly. It was dated August 12 of the previous year, and the headline read: "Disappointing Sales at Fairfield Yearling Auction."

Noah leaned over her shoulder. "Looks like an article about last year's auction."

"Fairfield yearling auction," Nancy said slowly. She stared up at Noah. "Your last name is Fairfield, right? Any relation?"

Noah straightened up. "It's my father's business," he replied a little stiffly.

"Jimmy's working on an article about this year's auction for the *Sentinel*," Eileen explained. "You know, sort of an informational piece: who'll be there, what yearlings are up for sale, stuff like that."

Nancy looked thoughtful. "Is it possible that he went off to pursue a lead in connection with his article and got sidetracked somehow?" she asked Eileen and Noah.

"That's definitely a possibility," Noah said. "I know Jimmy's been interviewing a lot of people about the auction. Maybe one of them gave him a hot tip."

His eyes lit up, and he grabbed Nancy's hands in his. "Hey, I have a plan. My old man is throwing a party at his house tonight, sort of a kickoff for the auction, which starts on Saturday. All the major players will be there—buyers, sellers, the press, you name it. Why don't you come with me, Nancy? You can do your detective thing and talk to people, see if anyone knows anything about Jimmy."

Nancy looked down at Noah's hands holding her own. Boy, this guy moves fast! she thought.

She gently withdrew her hands and gave Noah what she hoped was a cool but friendly smile. "That's a terrific idea," she told him. "I'd love to go." She turned to Eileen and George. "You guys are coming, too, right? I'll need your help."

"Um, sure," George said, glancing at Noah.

"I was supposed to go with Jimmy, anyway," Eileen added wistfully.

"Uh, well, great," Noah said. Nancy could tell that he was trying to mask his disappointment about having George and Eileen come along. "It's settled, then. I'll pick you all up at six. Oh, and by the way, it's black tie."

The *Saratoga Sentinel* office was located in an old mill building at the south end of Broadway. Inside, Nancy and George found a bored-looking receptionist sitting behind a large metal desk.

"Hi," Nancy said to her. "My name is Nancy Drew, and this is George Fayne. We'd like to speak to Jimmy English's boss."

"You mean Mavis?" The receptionist said. "Hang on." She picked up a phone, punched in a number, then spoke briefly. "Someone'll be right out," she said, hanging up. "Have a seat."

Nancy and George sat down on some folding

chairs. "It's probably just as well that Eileen had to head over to the coffeehouse," George murmured to Nancy. "Maybe work will help her get her mind off Jimmy."

"I don't know," Nancy said doubtfully. "She's really upset."

"What are you going to ask this Mavis person, anyway?" George asked.

"Well, for starters, I want to find out if Jimmy was working on any other articles besides the yearling auction piece," Nancy replied.

A set of double doors opened, and a girl in her late teens appeared. She was short and stocky, with waist-length black hair and a tawny complexion. She was wearing a red dress that looked several years out of fashion.

Her brown eyes settled on Nancy and George, as if sizing them up. "Hi," she said in a crisp, businesslike voice. "I'm Tracy Kim. Mavis is a little tied up right now. Can I help you with something?"

Nancy introduced herself and George. "Are you Mavis's assistant?" she asked Tracy.

"Actually, Mavis's assistant is out sick," Tracy replied. "I'm an intern, and I'm filling in."

"We're here to ask some questions about Jimmy English," George told Tracy. "He seems to be missing, and his fiancée asked us to help her find him."

Tracy arched her eyebrows. "Well, if you find

him," she said coolly, "you'd better turn him over to the police right away."

Nancy started. "What?"

Tracy nodded gravely. "We just discovered that our petty cash is missing. Jimmy is our prime suspect!"

Chapter
Three

NANCY COULDN'T BELIEVE what she was hearing. Jimmy a thief? she thought. It wasn't possible!

"Mavis is in her office with a couple of police officers right now," Tracy went on. "She's really upset about all this."

"I don't understand," Nancy said, frowning. "Why is Jimmy your prime suspect?"

"Are you friends of Jimmy and Eileens?" Tracy asked suspiciously.

"Yes," George replied.

"I guess it's okay to tell you, then," Tracy said. She sat down in a folding chair across from Nancy and George. "First of all, there's the timing. The money was there as of yesterday at six. So was Jimmy. Now he's gone, and so is the money."

"What time did he leave the office last night?" George asked Tracy.

"Around seven, according to Mavis," Tracy replied.

"The timing could be a coincidence," Nancy said slowly. "Just because Jimmy is missing doesn't mean he took the money."

Tracy looked uncomfortable. "Well, there's something else," she said, glancing over her shoulder. The only other person in the reception area was the receptionist, who was busy talking on the phone.

Tracy leaned forward in her chair. "There's the business of Jimmy's gambling problem," she said in a low voice. "There wasn't a lot of money in petty cash, but if he was desperate enough, he could have taken it to help pay off his gambling debts."

"Gambling problem?" Nancy repeated dumbly. "Jimmy has a gambling problem?"

"Well, we're not totally sure about it," Tracy said, "but it's a strong possibility. People have seen him talking to Popeye Lopez. I saw Jimmy talking to him myself."

"Who's Popeye Lopez?" George asked her.

"He's a bookie," Tracy explained. "You know, a guy who'll place bets for you for horse races, boxing matches, stuff like that. He used to work as a stablehand, but I guess he got greedy."

"Maybe Jimmy was working on a story about bookies," Nancy suggested.

Tracy shook her head. "Nope. The only article Jimmy's working on is the one about the upcoming yearling auction. So why's he having conversations with Popeye Lopez, unless he's doing business with him?"

Nancy was silent as she tried to absorb what Tracy was telling her. Having several conversations with a bookie didn't automatically make Jimmy a gambler—or a thief. But on the other hand, she could see how Jimmy's employers might suspect him. The timing of his disappearance, plus the fact that he'd been seen with a bookie, didn't look good.

"Can you tell me where I can find this Popeye Lopez?" she asked Tracy.

Tracy looked surprised. "Y-you're going to talk to him about this?" she stammered. "But why?"

"I just want to ask him a few questions," Nancy replied vaguely. She didn't want to discuss a case with someone she hardly knew.

Tracy was silent for a moment, as though she were considering something. "You could try the track," she said finally. "There's also the Palomino Grill. It's near the track, and I hear a lot of the bookies hang out there." Suddenly Tracy jumped up. "I'd better go. Mavis will be wondering where I am."

Nancy thought that Tracy seemed agitated all of a sudden. She wondered why. "One more thing," Nancy said. "Would it be possible to talk to some of Jimmy's other coworkers? I want to see if any of them might have some information about him."

"Maybe another day," Tracy said quickly. "This isn't a good time, with the police being here and all." Then she bid the girls goodbye and disappeared through the double doors.

George turned to Nancy, a troubled expression on her face. "If Tracy's right about Jimmy, Eileen is going to be totally devastated."

"I'm not convinced Tracy *is* right," Nancy told George. "I know it looks bad for Jimmy, but there's no solid evidence that he stole the petty cash or that he's a gambler." She stood up and dangled the keys to Eileen's car. Their friend had let them borrow it since she had to work. They had agreed to return it later to her at Lulu's. "Come on, Fayne, let's head over to the Palomino Grill. It's time for lunch—and a little talk with Popeye Lopez."

The Palomino Grill was like something out of an old movie. It was small, dark, and dingy, with a dozen leather booths and a few chrome tables. Behind the long wooden bar, Nancy noticed a television set, a couple of jockeys' jerseys, and photographs of famous racehorses.

Nancy and George sat down at a table. Nancy looked around. She and George appeared to be the only ones there.

"I'm starving," George murmured, picking up one of the menus that was on the table. "I had no idea it was so late."

"We've had kind of a busy morning," Nancy reminded her with a grin. She picked up a menu, too, and began reading it.

A few minutes later, a waiter approached their table. He seemed to be about eighty years old and was dressed in a short-sleeved white shirt, black pants, and a black bow tie. His gnarled fingers shook as he scribbled something onto a pad of paper.

He glanced up after a moment. "What'll ya have, girls?" he asked them.

"I'll have the Final Stretch Fish Sandwich and a ginger ale," George answered.

"I'll have the Winner's Circle Chicken Salad Plate and a seltzer," Nancy said.

The waiter frowned and peered over his shoulder. "Lucky for you, we still have a little chicken salad left. Big crowd came in before the first race and wiped us out."

Nancy handed him her menu. "Listen, we're looking for someone named Popeye Lopez. Have you seen him around?"

The waiter stared at her curiously. "Popeye Lopez? What do you want him for?"

"We just want to talk to him," George said casually.

"Well . . . haven't seen him today," the waiter said after a moment. "You want me to leave him a message? If I see him, I'll be glad to pass it along."

"Um, no," Nancy replied. "I'll try to find him some other way." She added, "Do you have a phone book here?"

"I'll get you one right away," the waiter offered. He tucked his pad into his shirt pocket and shuffled off toward the kitchen.

George turned to Nancy. "What if we don't find this Popeye Lopez? Then what?"

"Then we focus on getting some new leads at the party tonight," Nancy said. "Plus, if Jimmy hasn't turned up by the time we get home from the party, I'll suggest to Eileen that she file a missing persons report with the police."

"The police might be able to track Jimmy's car down," George pointed out. "That would be a huge help."

The waiter returned with a phone book and the girls' drinks.

"Do you happen to know Popeye's real name?" Nancy asked him.

The waiter frowned and shrugged. "Everyone always calls him Popeye."

After he left, Nancy flipped to the *L* section of the phone book. "Looman, Loomis, Loper," she murmured, her fingers trailing down the page. "Here it is, Lopez." She took a pen out of her shoulder bag and began writing on a paper napkin. "There's an Alvaro Lopez on Phila, and an M. Lopez on Division."

"Maybe one of them is Popeye, or a relative," George said. "Let's give them a call after lunch."

"Speaking of after lunch," Nancy said, taking a sip of her seltzer, "I have to buy a dress for tonight. I didn't bring anything fancy enough for a black-tie party."

"Me, either," George said, then made a face. "Clothes shopping—my least favorite activity."

"Oh, come on, it'll be fun," Nancy said cheerfully. "Besides, if we're going to mingle with Saratoga's rich and famous, we have to look the part."

The Fairfield estate was located in a beautiful rural area on the outskirts of Saratoga. As Noah turned his black convertible down the long, tree-lined driveway, George let out a low whistle. "Wow! You grew up here?"

"More or less," Noah replied. "I also did the boarding school thing in London, Paris, and Zurich." He grinned and added, "They kept kicking me out, so finally my parents let me come home and go to Saratoga High. Of course, the teachers there weren't so crazy about me, either. . . ."

As Noah talked, Nancy gazed at the scenery.

On either side of the driveway she saw acres and acres of rolling green pastures with horses grazing on them. The late afternoon sun made everything look golden.

At the end of the driveway was an enormous, white Greek Revival house with long, graceful columns. Beyond the house Nancy could see big striped tents and hundreds of people milling around.

Eileen turned to George. The two of them were sitting in the backseat while Nancy was sitting up front with Noah. "I'm not sure I'm up for a party," Eileen said softly.

Nancy overheard her friend, turned, and patted Eileen's hand. "You'll be fine," she said reassuringly. "Remember, this is all part of the plan to find Jimmy."

When they reached the house, Noah lined the car up behind two stretch limousines, a Rolls-Royce, and a Jaguar. After a moment, a parking valet came hurrying over to them. Noah stepped out, handed him the keys, and helped Eileen, George, and Nancy out of the car.

His hand lingered on Nancy's arm. "Did I tell you that you look totally gorgeous in that dress?" he said to her in a low voice. "Blue is definitely your color."

"Thanks," Nancy said with a smile. She glanced down at her short turquoise dress with spaghetti straps. "My boyfriend likes me in blue, too."

"You have a boyfriend, huh?" Noah said. "I should have figured someone like you would be taken." He grinned, seemingly unfazed by that fact, then led the way toward the tents in back of the house.

The party was in full swing. Under one tent a band was playing a fifties rock number near a dance floor mobbed with people. Under another tent a huge buffet table was set up opposite a bar. Waiters moved through the crowd, serving glasses of champagne and hors d'oeuvres. Nancy recognized some well-known models, actors, and politicians among the guests.

"Noah!"

Nancy glanced around. A tall man in his late forties was walking briskly toward their group. He had short, grayish blond hair, chiseled features, and silver, wire-rimmed glasses. Like most of the other men there, he was dressed in a black tuxedo.

The man approached Noah. "I see you made it," he said quietly.

Nancy looked at Noah, who suddenly looked very tense.

Noah turned to Nancy and her friends. "Nancy, George, and Eileen—this is my father, Oliver Fairfield," he said coolly. "Father, this is Nancy Drew, George Fayne, and Eileen Reed. Eileen is my roommate's fiancée."

With icy blue eyes, Mr. Fairfield regarded Eileen. "You're marrying Jimmy English, are you?" he murmured. "Well, congratulations. Have you set a date?"

"Um, yes," Eileen said, her eyes filling with tears. "The Saturday after Thanksgiving. But the thing is—the thing is—" Her voice broke.

"Jimmy is missing," Nancy broke in, putting her hand on Eileen's arm. "No one's heard from him in the last twenty-four hours. In fact, we were wondering if you might have some information about him."

Mr. Fairfield raised his eyebrows. "Me? Goodness, no. Really, it sounds more like a matter for the police, Miss Drew."

"Jimmy was working on an article about your auction," George said. "Did he interview you for it?"

"Yes," Mr. Fairfield replied, looking surprised. "Why?"

"Is it possible that Jimmy went off to pursue a lead in connection with his article and got sidetracked somehow?" Nancy asked him.

"I can't imagine," Mr. Fairfield said with a small laugh. "As far as I can tell, his article was going to be of a strictly informational nature. It was hardly an exposé that might involve *leads* or anything of that sort."

His eyes drifted past Nancy. "Excuse me, won't you?" he asked pleasantly. "The mayor and her husband have just arrived, and I must say hello. It was nice meeting you all. I do wish you luck in finding young Mr. English." He glanced at Noah and added, "Perhaps we can talk later?"

Noah shrugged. "Sure. Whatever."

As soon as his father had left, Noah turned to Nancy. "Care to dance?" he asked. He was smiling, but Nancy could see that he was tense. She wondered about Noah's relationship with his father. Had something happened between them recently to trigger Noah's anxious reaction?

"Um, why don't you dance with George?" Nancy said, thinking quickly. "Eileen and I need to go to the ladies' room. Come on, Eileen." Before Noah or George could say anything, Nancy grabbed Eileen by the elbow and steered her in the direction of the main house.

Nancy paused when they reached a semi-secluded spot near the side of the house. "Are you okay?" Nancy asked, her voice gentle with concern.

"As okay as I can be under the circumstances." Eileen said.

"I think you're doing great," Nancy said. She hoped Eileen was going to be able to deal with what she had to say. "Listen, this is the first chance I've had to talk to you alone. I wanted you to know that George and I went by the *Sentinel* after we left you this morning."

Eileen perked up. "And? Did you find something out about Jimmy?"

Nancy took a deep breath, then said, "Petty

cash is missing from their office. An intern named Tracy Kim told me that Jimmy is a suspect."

"What!" Eileen burst out. "That is way off base! Jimmy would *never* steal money!"

"I couldn't see it, either," Nancy agreed. "But there's more. Tracy suggested that Jimmy might have a gambling problem. Apparently, people have seen him talking to a bookie named Popeye Lopez."

"Jimmy does *not* have a gambling problem," Eileen said emphatically. "He doesn't steal, and he doesn't gamble." She gave an odd little laugh. "You don't understand. Jimmy is totally honest. He told me once that he's never lied in his life. He can't stand liars. So why would he suddenly develop this secret life?"

"I don't know," Nancy murmured. She felt bad sharing Tracy's suspicions about Jimmy with Eileen, but she needed to learn Eileen's feelings. "I tried to find Popeye Lopez this afternoon," Nancy went on. "I even called the two Lopezes who are in the phone book. But neither of them knew Popeye."

"I've never heard of this Popeye person," Eileen said. She twirled one of her rhinestone earrings around and stared off into space. "I wonder—" Then she stopped talking and began waving wildly at someone. "Sean! Oh, Sean, I'm so glad you're here!" she called out.

Nancy turned around. A tall, burly man in his

early thirties was coming toward them. He had curly red hair, a mustache, and a beard. He was dressed in a black tuxedo with a tie-dyed cummerbund, red socks, and leather sandals. Nancy thought his outfit was fun, although he looked out of place at the conservative gathering.

Eileen ran up to him and gave him a hug. Then she turned to Nancy. "Nancy, this is my brother Sean," she said. "Sean, this is my friend Nancy Drew. I met her on my camping trip in Vermont."

Sean extended a hand to Nancy. "Nice to meet you, Nancy," he said warmly. "Enjoying the party?"

"Well—" Nancy began.

"Oh, Sean," Eileen suddenly cut in, grabbing his arm. "Jimmy's missing. He's been missing since last night!"

Sean looked shocked. "What?"

"And some petty cash is missing from the newspaper office, and people there are saying he might have taken it and disappeared," Eileen babbled on. "Can you believe it? They're even saying that he might have a secret gambling problem, and that's why he took the money. Just because he was seen talking to some bookie named Popeye Lopez! Big deal!"

Nancy glanced at Sean. She noticed a strange expression cross his face. Maybe he's just surprised at learning Jimmy might be a gambler, Nancy thought.

Eileen let go of Sean's arm and pulled Nancy closer. "Nancy's a detective, and she's helping me find Jimmy," Eileen finished.

"I'm glad for you, honey, but have you thought about calling the police?" Sean asked her with concern.

"I think that's going to be our next step," Nancy told him.

Just then, a waiter came up to her. "Excuse me, are you Nancy Drew?"

Nancy nodded. "Yes."

"A gentleman wishes to speak to you in the library," the waiter informed her. "If you go in through the front of the house, it's the second door to your left."

Nancy frowned. "Who is it?"

"He didn't give me a name," the waiter replied.

Nancy thought of Noah. "Is he tall with longish blond hair?" she asked him.

The waiter shook his head. "No, he has dark hair."

"Hmm," Nancy said, perplexed. "Well, I guess I'll go see what he wants." She turned to Eileen. "I'll catch up with you later, okay? And, Sean, it was nice meeting you," she added.

"Same here," Sean said amiably.

Nancy walked around the house to the front door and entered. She found herself in a large, magnificently furnished foyer. A beautiful painting of a woman on horseback hung over an ornate Victorian table. The marble floor was covered with a long oriental runner in shades of blue and red.

Nancy admired the painting for a moment, then proceeded down the hall to the second door on the left. It was closed.

She knocked on it softly. "Hello?" she called out. There was no answer.

Puzzled, Nancy opened the door and went into the library. The room was empty. "That's strange," she murmured.

But just as she was turning to leave, she was startled by a sudden movement behind her. Nancy felt a chill of fear: she realized that someone was sneaking up on her. Before she could react, she felt a hand clamping firmly over her mouth.

Chapter

Four

"FANCY MEETING YOU here," a voice murmured in her ear.

Nancy gasped, then whirled around. She took in the tall, handsome guy with dark hair, big brown eyes, a drop-dead smile . . .

"Frank Hardy!" Nancy exclaimed. She threw her arms around him and hugged him. Frank hugged her back. "I'm sorry about the sneaky way I got you to come to the library," he apologized. "I saw you out the window, and I couldn't resist. It's not often I have a chance to put something over on you."

Nancy laughed. "It's okay," she told him, closing her eyes and enjoying being in his arms. He and his younger brother, Joe, were old friends of hers. Like Nancy, the Hardys were both detectives.

There had always been a little more than friendship between her and Frank. But because Nancy had a boyfriend and Frank had a girlfriend, their relationship had never gone anywhere.

Nancy stepped back and gave Frank the once-over. He was dressed in a charcoal gray tuxedo and an elegant white shirt with no tie. "Nice tux," she said approvingly. "So, what are you doing here?"

"I could ask you the same question," Frank said with a grin. "Either you're doing the August in Saratoga thing, or you're on a case."

"Actually, it's both." Nancy hooked her arm through his. "Come on, let's sit, and I'll tell you all about it."

They settled down on one of the couches, and Nancy proceeded to fill him in on the events of the last few days. "So that's the story," she finished. "Anyway, Jimmy's roommate, Noah, suggested that we come to this party in case someone here might have some information about Jimmy. So far, the only person we've talked to is Mr. Fairfield, Noah's father. And he wasn't much help."

"Mr. Oliver Cox Fairfield the Third?" Frank said, looking amused. "I'm surprised you managed to pin him down long enough to talk. He's a busy guy."

Nancy leaned forward. "How do you know him?"

"He hired Joe and me and a bunch of other people to work security for the yearling auction this Saturday," Frank replied. "And for all the stuff leading up to it, like this party."

"What does he need security for?" Nancy asked.

"To keep an eye on the yearlings, for one thing." Frank paused to adjust one of his pearl cuff links. "There's an incredibly valuable yearling up for sale, so Mr. Fairfield wanted extra security. His name is Goldenrod, and he's expected to sell for two million dollars or more."

"George read something about Goldenrod in the paper," Nancy told Frank. "So why is he so valuable?"

"He's the foal of Golden Folly, who's one of the most important horses in racing history," Frank replied. "She won the Triple Crown several times. No one could beat her. Anyway, Goldenrod is her first and only foal. Golden Folly died in labor when she gave birth to him."

Nancy whistled. "Wow. No wonder Goldenrod's such a big deal."

Frank nodded. "People have come from all over the world to bid on Goldenrod this Saturday—another reason for the high security."

Frank rose to his feet and walked over to a large bay window. "I need to keep an eye on what's happening." Nancy joined him at the window.

"Check this out," Frank said. "See that guy over there?" He pointed to a slim, dark-haired man who was walking purposefully across the lawn. "That's Marco Donatelli, the Italian race car driver. And that"—he indicated a young guy with a ponytail—"is Luke Ventura, the actor."

"We saw him at the track yesterday morning," Nancy said. "He wants to buy Goldenrod?"

"Yup. Him and Donatelli, plus several others; the prince of Morocco, an oil baron from Texas named Wyatt Vaughn, and a French business-woman named Brigitte Bouvier," Frank rattled off. "They all tried to make preemptive bids on Goldenrod, but Mr. Fairfield wouldn't let them. It's against house rules. So now they're in Saratoga for the auction."

"Very interesting," Nancy murmured. She pointed to Sean, who was now talking to a paunchy, middle-aged man. Eileen was nowhere in sight. "By the way, see that big red-haired guy? That's Eileen's brother Sean."

"Oh, yeah, I saw you talking to him," Frank said. "Did you know he's a vet? I've seen him at the Fairfield paddocks, taking care of some of the yearlings. And see the guy he's with? That's Abe Addison of Addison Farms, Goldenrod's owner."

"And soon to be a multimillionaire if Golden-rod goes for a high price," Nancy remarked.

"Definitely," Frank said. Then he scanned the crowd. "Hmm, I wonder where Joe is? I haven't seen him in a while. We split up so that we could circulate better."

"Knowing Joe, he's probably circulating out on the dance floor," Nancy said, smiling.

Joe Hardy munched on a carrot stick and frowned at the band. The song they were playing was a cross between oldies rock and easy listening: definitely not his style. Everybody seemed to be into the band, though. The dance floor was a mob scene.

He tossed the remainder of his carrot stick into a nearby wastebasket. He decided to get some *real* food at the buffet table.

As he made his way to the tent where the buffet table was, he happened to spot two familiar faces: the race car driver Marco Donatelli and the Frenchwoman Brigitte Bouvier. They were hovering just outside the dance tent and seemed to be having an intense conversation. Joe's blue eyes lingered for a moment on Brigitte. In her thirties, she was an incredibly beautiful woman. She wore her long, honey blond hair up, with wisps falling loosely around her face. Her elegant black cocktail dress complemented her slim figure.

Joe wondered what she and Marco were talking about. Mr. Fairfield had asked him and Frank to attend his party posing as guests to "keep an eye on things," whatever that meant. The conversation between Brigitte and Marco seemed as though it was on the verge of erupting into an argument.

Just then somebody tapped him on the shoulder. "Excuse me, but you're blocking my way."

Joe whirled around, mentally preparing to get into an argument of his own. He was surprised to see George Fayne standing behind him, grinning broadly.

"George!" he said happily. He gave her a big hug. "I don't believe it! Don't tell me. You came into an inheritance, and you're in town to buy ponies."

"Oh, yeah, right," George said, laughing. "Actually, Nancy and I are here on vacation." She lowered her voice and added, "We're also trying to help out a friend. Her fiancé's disappeared."

"That's a bummer," Joe murmured. "Did he get cold feet about marriage or something?"

"I think it's more complicated than that," George replied dryly. She reached over and straightened Joe's bow tie. "So what about you? What are you doing here, all duded up in a tux?"

Joe glanced down at his outfit and grimaced. "This penguin suit?" he said. "Believe me, I wouldn't be wearing it if it wasn't part of the job." Then he explained to George how he and Frank had been hired by Oliver Fairfield.

"A lot of people want to buy this yearling,

Goldenrod," Joe finished. "The prince of Morocco, Luke Ventura—"

"Luke Ventura?" George cut in. "We saw him while we were having breakfast at the track yesterday. I was so psyched. He's one of my favorite actors."

Joe glanced over her shoulder. "Well, you can tell him so yourself. Don't look now, but he's heading our way."

George spun around. Luke Ventura was walking up to them. He introduced himself to George and Joe, then fixed his green eyes on George. "Um, I was wondering if you might want to dance," he said. He sounded almost shy.

"You—want—to—dance?" George repeated slowly. "Um, sure, great. I'd love to." She threw Joe a radiant smile and extended a hand to Luke.

"Have fun, kids," Joe said, giving them a minisalute. "Okay, now, what was I doing?" he asked himself. "Oh, yeah—food." He started purposefully toward the buffet tent.

When he got there, he couldn't decide where to begin. There were enormous platters of cheeses, patés, and breads. Plus, there were stuffed mushrooms, little quiches, melon wrapped with prosciutto, sushi, shrimp cocktail, a dozen different kinds of olives, and more.

Joe grabbed a plate and began piling it high with food. He'd skipped lunch that day, and he was starving. He made sure to get extra shrimp cocktail. He loved the spicy sauce.

But just as he turned to leave the table, someone ran into him, knocking his plate out of his hands. "Oh, great," he muttered as food flew everywhere.

A short, pretty girl with long auburn hair was glaring at him. She looked to be about sixteen years old. Her pink dress was covered with red cocktail sauce.

"See what you did?" she cried in a thick southern accent.

Joe couldn't believe his ears. "What *I* did? *You* bumped into *me.*"

The girl's dark brown eyes blazed angrily. "Well, if you think that, you're crazy. You ran into me and spilled shrimp cocktail all over my new dress!"

"I'm sorry about your dress," Joe said patiently. "But I didn't do it. I was standing here minding my own business when you plowed into me like a linebacker—"

The girl gasped. "I've never met anyone as rude as you," she told him huffily. "Wait till I tell Daddy about what you did. He'll sue you!" She turned on her heel and stormed off.

Joe shook his head as he watched her walk away. What a brat, he thought. On the other hand, what a cute brat, he amended.

Joe started to make another plate for himself. At the same moment a piercing scream broke through the air. He dropped the plate and turned in the direction of the scream.

The other party guests were looking around in confusion. "What on earth was that?" an elderly woman asked Joe.

But Joe didn't have time to reply. His senses on full alert, he rushed out of the tent ahead of some other guests. Just then, another scream rang out. This time Joe could tell that it was coming from the rose garden behind the house.

He took off. In the garden, he found Brigitte Bouvier, standing behind a high trellis of climbing roses and sobbing hysterically.

"What's going on?" Joe asked her.

But Brigitte didn't have to tell him. She glanced down, and Joe followed her glance. Lying on the ground, surrounded by pink and yellow rose petals, was Marco Donatelli.

Joe tried to stifle his shock. There was a knife sticking out of Marco Donatelli's back.

Chapter

Five

BRIGITTE RUSHED UP to Joe and clutched his arm. "I am so thankful you are here," she cried out. Her voice was low and throaty, and she had a heavy French accent. "I do not know what to do. I have never seen a—a dead man." She looked as though she were about to faint.

Joe patted her shoulder reassuringly, then turned to one of the people who had just arrived at the scene. "You," Joe called out. "Yeah, you. Go to the house and call 911. *Now!*" The guy nodded and ran off.

Joe knelt down on the ground and felt for a pulse at Marco's neck. There was none. He was definitely dead.

"Oh boy," Joe muttered.

"Joe! What's going on?"

Joe peered over his shoulder and saw Frank and Nancy. He wanted to say hi to Nancy—it had been a while since he'd seen her—but now was not the time to catch up with old friends. "Murder victim," Joe explained hastily. "It's Marco Donatelli. I just sent someone to call the police."

Oliver Fairfield appeared a moment later, breathing heavily. He took in the sight of Marco's body and gasped. "Oh, dear. Oh, *dear!* Is that Mr. Donatelli?" he demanded.

"Yes, sir," Joe told him. "Ms. Bouvier found him."

"I think everybody should clear out of here until the police get here," Nancy said loudly. "We don't want to disturb any evidence."

Everybody filed out of the rose garden. Mr. Fairfield took a cellular phone out of his pocket, punched in some numbers, then spoke rapidly into the phone. "Henry? Tell the band to make an announcement to the guests that everything is all right. Ask them to play something loud— anything. And serve extra champagne. Get on it!"

Brigitte dabbed her eyes with a lace handkerchief. "I was coming out to the garden to see Monsieur Fairfield's famous roses," she said to Joe. "And then I saw—I saw poor Monsieur Donatelli lying there like that. I thought at first that it was some horrible trick, a prank, but then

I realized . . ." Her voice trailed off, and she began crying again.

"It's okay," Joe told her, patting her on the shoulder again. He glanced helplessly at Frank. Frank shrugged.

A short while later, four police officers arrived. One of them, who introduced herself as Lieutenant Carol Goldberg, asked questions while the other three examined the body and the crime scene.

When she learned that Brigitte had found the body, Lieutenant Goldberg began to ask her some questions. "Approximately what time did you discover the victim?" she asked Brigitte.

"I am not sure," Brigitte replied. "Perhaps thirty minutes ago."

"I can verify that," Joe spoke up. "That's when we all heard her scream, anyway."

Lieutenant Goldberg nodded. "And did you know the victim, Ms. Bouvier?"

Brigitte shook her head. "No, not at all."

Joe did a double take. "What?" he sputtered. "But I saw the two of you talking earlier, right outside the dance tent. It looked like a pretty heavy discussion."

Brigitte's large gray eyes widened. "You saw . . . oh, you saw *that*," she murmured, waving her hand dismissively. "Monsieur Donatelli was—how do you say it—flirting with me. He wanted me to dance with him. I was not interested, and so I asked him to please leave me alone. He was very persistent," she added.

"And was that the last time you saw him this evening?" Lieutenant Goldberg asked her.

"Yes, until—until—" Brigitte pointed shakily at the rose garden.

Joe stared at Brigitte thoughtfully. He wondered if she was being totally up front with Lieutenant Goldberg. The conversation he'd witnessed earlier hadn't seemed like romantic bantering. On the other hand, maybe Marco had been hitting on her in a decidedly unromantic way, and Brigitte had become angry.

Lieutenant Goldberg scribbled something on a pad, then looked up and addressed Mr. Fairfield. "I'm going to call for reinforcements. Everyone at this party is going to have to be interviewed, just in case someone might have seen something important. I don't want any of your guests to leave. Is that understood?"

"Very well," Mr. Fairfield said with a sigh. "However, please ask your men to treat my guests with respect. Many of them are VIPs."

"My men and women will do what they can," Lieutenant Goldberg said. "Just keep in mind," she added pointedly, "that one of your VIPs might turn out to be a murderer."

Joe glanced over at Frank, who was looking grim. Joe knew exactly what his brother was thinking: their jobs had just become much more difficult. Providing security for the yearling auction with a murderer on the loose was definitely *not* going to be fun and games.

Especially if the murderer had any ideas about striking again.

Later that evening, Nancy found Eileen and George sitting at a table in the dance tent, nursing a couple of ginger ales. The place was nearly deserted; the band had packed up hours ago, and most of the guests were gone as well. The sky was dark and thick with stars, and the air was filled with the sound of crickets.

Nancy pulled out a folding chair and sat down wearily. "What a night," she murmured.

"What a night is right," George said. "Where have you been?"

"Well, for a while, Frank and Joe and I were tagging along with the police while they interviewed the guests," Nancy explained.

"Did you pick up anything?" Eileen asked.

"Not too much," Nancy replied. "None of the guests had any information about Marco or his murderer. A forensics expert is examining Marco's body for trace evidence, though. Maybe he'll be able to learn something."

George took a sip of her ginger ale. "Were there any fingerprints on the knife?"

Nancy shook her head. "They'd been wiped clean." She added, "The knife belonged to the caterers. The police think that the murderer stole it from the buffet table."

Eileen shuddered. "This whole thing is too gruesome."

"So the police have no suspects, huh?" George asked Nancy.

"None whatsoever." Nancy glanced over her shoulder. "By the way, have either of you guys seen Noah lately? I've been looking all over for him."

"Noah?" George repeated. "Hmm. Come to think of it, I haven't seen him since we got here."

"Neither have I," Eileen said.

Nancy frowned. "That's so weird. *I* haven't seen him, either. Maybe he left the party— although I can't *believe* he'd leave without us. That would be incredibly rude. How does he expect us to get back?"

Frank and Joe showed up just then. Joe was dangling car keys from his hand. "We're outta here," he announced. He fixed his eyes on Eileen and smiled. "Hi, I'm Joe Hardy."

"Eileen Reed," she said, extending a hand.

Frank introduced himself as well. "You guys need a ride home?" he asked.

"Actually, I think we do," Nancy replied. "Noah seems to have disappeared."

The five of them walked out to the parking area. Nancy saw that there were only a few cars left and that Noah's black convertible was not one of them.

"He's definitely gone," Nancy said.

"That's so bizarre," George remarked. "I mean, why would Noah ditch us like that?"

Frank looked thoughtful as he opened the doors to his and Joe's van. "When was the last time you guys saw Noah?"

"Not since the beginning of the party," Nancy said, sliding into the backseat. Eileen and George scooted in next to her.

Frank got into the driver's seat and turned to look at Nancy. "Okay, so, suppose he *did* leave way back then. That's kind of weird, isn't it? I mean, it's his father's party, and he did bring the three of you with him, right?" He added, "Tell me—did Noah know Marco Donatelli?"

Nancy stared at Frank, her blue eyes wide. She couldn't believe what he was implying. "Are you suggesting that *Noah* might have had something to do with Marco's murder?" she demanded.

Frank turned forward and started the van. "I'm just throwing out a theory," he said with a shrug. "I mean, how well do you know this guy?"

Nancy was silent. When it came right down to it, she didn't know Noah at all, except for the fact that he was cute and unemployed, and had been kicked out of several boarding schools. Could he really be a cold-blooded killer?

"I know Noah pretty well," Eileen spoke up. "And I can't imagine him murdering someone, although he does have a major temper problem. But still, I don't think he would ever hurt anyone."

The five of them continued to discuss Marco's murder until they reached the downtown area. Broadway was bustling: the outdoor cafés were packed, street musicians were playing on the sidewalk, and there were lines of people waiting to get into the clubs. Nancy loved the ambiance of Saratoga: the combination of old-fashioned Victorian elegance and cosmopolitan charm.

Eileen leaned forward in her seat. "Can you drop me off at the police station?" she asked Frank. "It's right over there." She turned to Nancy. "I'm taking your suggestion and filing a missing persons report on Jimmy."

"Good," Nancy said. "Do you want George and me to come with you?"

Eileen shook her head. "I'll be fine. You guys get some sleep. I'll call you in the morning and tell you how it went."

Frank stopped the van in front of the police station, and Eileen stepped out. She smiled at the Hardys. "It was nice meeting you guys. Thanks for the ride."

"No problem," Joe said with a wave.

Frank started the van again and continued down Broadway, toward Nancy and George's hotel. Once there, he parked the van and glanced over his shoulder at Nancy. "So what's your next move in your search for Eileen's fiancé?" he asked her.

"Well, having her file a missing persons report should help," Nancy replied. "The police can try to track down Jimmy's car. Plus," she added, "I thought George and I might go to the races tomorrow afternoon and look for Popeye Lopez. Since he's a bookie, I don't think we'll have trouble finding someone who knows him and can point him out. I really want to ask him about Jimmy's so-called gambling habit."

"Well, we may see you there, then," Frank told her. "Mr. Fairfield invited some guests to his private box at the track, and we'll be there to keep an eye on things. Although maybe Mr. Fairfield will cancel, with the murder and everything."

"Our Mr. Fairfield call off the field trip to the track? No way," Joe said. "That would be bad PR, and he seems like a PR-conscious kind of guy."

Nancy and George said good night to the Hardys, then stepped out of the van. Inside the hotel there was a jazz quartet playing in the ornate lobby, and just beyond, a group of people were sitting at the zinc and marble bar.

Nancy stopped at the front desk to check for messages. The clerk reached into the box for Room 324 and pulled out a folded-up slip of paper. "Here you go," she said pleasantly.

Nancy unfolded it. It said: "Call Frederick Jones." There was no phone number listed.

"Frederick Jones?" Nancy said out loud. "I don't know any Frederick Jones." She frowned at the clerk. "Are you sure this is right?"

"I took the message myself," the clerk replied. "I'm sure that's what the man said—Frederick Jones. He called about an hour ago. He said you'd have his number."

"That's really weird," Nancy murmured. She stuffed the piece of paper into her handbag. "Oh, well. I'm sure he'll call again if he really needs to speak to me."

The two girls proceeded to the elevator bank. On the way, they saw someone familiar: Tracy Kim, the intern from the paper. Dressed in an expensive-looking black silk dress, she was coming out of the ladies' room and rooting through her purse for something.

"Hi, Tracy," Nancy called out with a smile. "What are you doing here?"

Tracy's head shot up. "Oh, hi," she said, snapping her purse shut. "I'm—well, I was meeting some friends here to listen to the jazz quartet, but I can't seem to find them, so I was just about to leave." Nancy thought she seemed flustered.

"Great outfit," Nancy said.

"Oh, thanks. Listen, I've got to run." Without saying goodbye, Tracy shot past them and into the lobby, toward the exit.

"Nice seeing you, too," George said dryly.

"She's definitely not the friendliest person in the world," Nancy agreed.

Nancy and George took the elevator up to the third floor, then went down the hall to their room. "It must be about midnight," Nancy said to George as she unlocked their door. "It feels like it's three in the morning, though. What a *long* night."

"We're definitely going to sleep well," George said, following Nancy through the door.

Nancy started to turn on the light, then hesitated. Her intuition told her that something was wrong. She scanned the dark room. She couldn't see anyone.

Still, she was wary. She stepped back toward the door, gesturing for George to do the same.

"Nan?" George asked softly. "What is it?"

"Stand back," Nancy whispered. "I'm going to turn the light on."

Nancy flicked on the switch. There was no one in the room. But it was clear that someone *had* been there.

A large chef's knife had been plunged into one of the pillows on Nancy's bed. Her heart racing, Nancy stepped forward to take a closer look. Attached to the knife was a note written in red ink, in a wild, childish scrawl:

STOP LOOKING FOR JIMMY
OR YOU'LL END UP LIKE MARCO!

Chapter

Six

GEORGE GASPED. "Nancy . . . someone—someone was in here," she stammered.

"Someone could *still* be here," Nancy replied tensely. Quickly she unplugged the heavy lamp on the nearby nightstand and picked the lamp up to use as a weapon. Then she moved quietly over to the bathroom, then opened the door quickly. There was no one inside. After handing the lamp to George to stand guard with, Nancy checked the closet and under both beds. She found no one.

Nancy took a deep breath. Her head was spinning. Who could have done this? she wondered.

"That knife and note are incredibly creepy," George said with a shudder.

Nancy sat down on the bed and examined the note closely. "The intruder must have been at the party tonight," she observed, glancing up at George. "Unless whoever it was found out about Marco's murder on TV."

"News like that travels fast," George pointed out, putting the lamp back on the nightstand. "After all, Marco was famous."

"That's true," Nancy agreed.

George sat down on the bed next to her friend. "Who would want you off this case so much?"

"I have no idea," Nancy replied. "But whoever it is really doesn't want Jimmy found. Which makes me think that his disappearance involves something much more important than the *Sentinel*'s missing petty cash."

Nancy spent the next few minutes searching the room for clues and checking for signs of forced entry. On the outside doorknob she discovered tiny scratches. "Looks like the person picked the lock," Nancy said. "I think it's time to call the hotel manager—and the police."

The hotel manager, Mr. Barsamian, came up as soon as Nancy phoned him. "I'm so sorry," he said when he saw the knife and the note. "We have never had an incident of this sort."

"How do you suppose the intruder discovered our room number?" Nancy asked him.

"It's very puzzling," Mr. Barsamian replied with a frown. "We have a strict policy against giving out our guests' room numbers." He added, "If a room opens up, I will be happy to move you. Until then, there will be no charge for your room."

Nancy was about to thank him when there was a knock on the door.

"I'll get it," Mr. Barsamian said. He opened the door.

"Sergeant John Aiello," a stocky, gray-haired police officer said brusquely. He poked his head into the room and glanced around. "You reported a break-in?"

"Yes, I did," Nancy told him. "Come on in. I'm Nancy Drew. This is my friend George Fayne and the hotel manager, Mr. Barsamian."

Nancy told Sergeant Aiello everything, beginning with Jimmy's disappearance and ending with her discovery of the knife and note. "Jimmy's fiancée, Eileen Reed, is down at the station as we speak," she finished. "She's filing a missing persons report."

Sergeant Aiello scribbled the information down. Then he looked up and said, "Are you aware that Jimmy English is a suspect in the petty cash theft at the *Sentinel*?"

"Yes, I'm aware of that," Nancy replied. "But as far as I know, there's no solid evidence that he stole the money."

Sergeant Aiello stared at the threatening note. "You know, it's possible that Mr. English wrote that note to throw you off track."

Nancy frowned. From what little she knew of

61

Jimmy, it didn't seem like something he would do. Besides, even if she conceded that Jimmy had stolen the money and taken off, why would he show up at the hotel and risk getting caught?

She pointed all this out to Sergeant Aiello. "Thieves are very clever people, Ms. Drew," he told her. "You have no idea how the criminal mind works."

"Actually—" George began.

Nancy shot her a look. She didn't want it known that she was a detective and that she was all too familiar with the criminal mind. George caught the look and immediately shut up.

Sergeant Aiello asked Nancy a few more questions. Then he proceeded to dust the doorknob for fingerprints. "I'm not getting anything," he said after a few minutes. "There are too many sets of prints, and they're all smudged. In any case, I'm taking the knife and note as evidence."

After saying he would keep Nancy posted, Sergeant Aiello left. Mr. Barsamian left as well, apologizing again to the girls and reiterating his offer of not charging them. He also promised that the hotel security guards would keep an eye out for any unusual activity on their floor.

"Some holiday," George said wearily. "First Jimmy disappears, then the murder, and now this . . ."

"Frederick Jones," Nancy said suddenly.

George frowned. "Huh?"

Nancy reached into her purse and pulled out

the phone message she'd retrieved at the front desk. "That's how the intruder found out our room number!"

"I'm *totally* not following you," George said.

"The intruder came into the hotel with a cellular phone," Nancy explained patiently. "He stood near the front desk somewhere and called the main number. When the clerk answered, he gave her a bogus message for me so he could see what box she put the slip of paper into. All the boxes are marked with the room numbers, remember?"

George's brown eyes widened. "Oh, yeah. Wow, that's pretty clever!"

"Clever is right," Nancy agreed. "The lobby was such a zoo tonight, I'm sure no one would have noticed him."

"Actually, we don't know that it's a *him,* right?" George reminded Nancy. "Our intruder could have been a woman."

"She would have had to disguise her voice as a man's," Nancy pointed out.

Then Nancy had the fleeting image of Tracy Kim coming out of the ladies' room downstairs, acting flustered and anxious. Could *she* have been the intruder? Nancy asked herself. But she couldn't imagine why the young intern would go to such lengths to keep Jimmy from being found.

Still, she had to consider Tracy a suspect on the grounds of opportunity alone, Nancy told herself. Plus, there was Popeye Lopez. Although she had no reason to think that he was involved in Jimmy's disappearance, he was a shadowy figure whose relationship with Jimmy was unclear. After all, he was a bookie, and he'd been seen talking to Jimmy recently.

And speaking of suspicious figures, there was also Noah. The fact that he'd left the party so mysteriously didn't look good.

Was Frank right? Nancy wondered apprehensively. Was there a chance that Noah was connected to Marco's murder—and Jimmy's disappearance, too?

The phone rang, jolting Nancy from her thoughts. "I'll get that," she told George.

Nancy walked over to the nightstand and picked up the phone. "Hello?"

"I see you got my note," said a male voice that Nancy didn't recognize. The man spoke in a hoarse whisper. "I just hope you'll be smart and do what it says. I'd hate to have to kill a pretty girl like you."

Chapter

Seven

A SHIVER OF FEAR went up Nancy's spine. She'd received threatening calls before, but this person's voice was especially menacing.

"Who is this?" she asked after a moment.

She heard a click, followed by the dial tone.

As Nancy hung up the phone, George stared at her. "Nan? Who was that?"

"It was the guy who left us the note and the knife," Nancy said slowly. She repeated his words to George.

"Did you recognize his voice?" George asked.

Nancy shook her head. "He was talking in a whisper, so it was hard to tell. But one thing's for sure. The guy means business. We're going to have to watch our backs on this case."

Then Nancy remembered something. While

the guy was talking, she'd heard a faint noise in the background: the sound of a woman singing a bluesy-sounding song. The singer had sounded like Billie Holiday. The guy must have been playing the radio or a CD, she told herself.

Suddenly Nancy's mind flashed back to her visit to Noah's apartment that morning. There had been a Billie Holiday song playing on his stereo.

No way, Nancy thought, startled. It must be a coincidence. But deep down, she couldn't deny this important clue. Things were beginning to look bad for Noah.

"I want to give you boys a new job," Mr. Fairfield told the Hardys.

It was Friday morning, and Joe and Frank were at Fairfield, Inc., for the presale paces. The yearlings to be sold at the next day's auction were stabled there. At the moment many of them were being led around the paddocks by handlers so that prospective buyers could see them in action.

Mr. Fairfield and the Hardys were standing a little way behind the crowd, drinking coffee. Mr. Fairfield watched a bay filly trot by, then fixed his icy blue eyes on the brothers. "I want you to find Marco Donatelli's murderer," he said quietly.

"You want us to find Marco Donatelli's murderer," Frank repeated slowly. "But the police are on that already."

"Yes, yes, I know that." Mr. Fairfield waved

his hand dismissively. "The police will do what they can, of course. But I would like to do something extra to see that this murderer is caught. And that's where the two of you come in."

Frank and Joe exchanged glances. Joe raised his eyebrows very slightly. Frank knew that expression well; it meant, "It's your call."

Frank turned his attention back to Mr. Fairfield. "We'll be glad to take on the job," he told the older man. "For starters, we'll need any information you have about Marco Donatelli. He's from Sicily, right?"

Mr. Fairfield nodded.

"We'll also need access to your guest list from last night," Joe added.

Just then a big, red-haired man came up to Mr. Fairfield. He was dressed in jeans and a blue T-shirt, and he was carrying a black leather bag. "Sorry to disturb you, Oliver, but there's a problem with Hip Number Forty-three. You want to take a look at her X-rays?"

Mr. Fairfield looked distracted. "Forty-three? Oh, yes. Excuse me, won't you?" he said to the Hardys. "I'll have my assistant, Benjamin, give you the information you need."

When he'd gone, Frank turned to Joe. "That was Eileen Reed's brother Sean. He's a vet."

"So I gathered," Joe replied. He made a face. "Is it just me, or does Hip Number Forty-three seem like a weird name for a horse?"

"A lot of these yearlings don't get named until they're bought by someone at the auction," Frank explained. "They're all given these things called hip numbers. It's a way of identifying them and listing them in the auction catalog."

"How do you manage to keep so much tedious trivia stored in that brain of yours?" Joe asked his brother with a grin. Then his grin disappeared. "Okay, let's get serious here. What are we going to do about catching Marco's killer?"

"We'll have to wait for the info from Mr. Fairfield's assistant," Frank said. "In the meantime, let's split up and wander around. We should scope out the people here, see if any of them knew Marco—or if any of them talked to him last night. We won't be able to cover everyone, but it'll be a start."

Joe threw his empty foam cup into a trash can. "Good plan. Let's meet back here in about an hour."

Joe wandered off in the direction of the stables. Frank took another sip of his coffee and glanced around, getting his bearings. The auction pavillion was on the southeastern corner of the large, grassy lot. The rest of the area consisted of the paddocks and many rows of stables. Frank knew that the buildings dated from the late nineteenth century. They were white with dark green trim and had signs with old-fashioned lettering on them.

There were people everywhere, watching the

yearlings in action, studying them close up, or just taking in the scene. Most of them were dressed casually in jeans and denim shirts, but Frank knew that they were probably millionaires. He'd seen the Jaguars and Rolls-Royces in the parking lot.

Then Frank spotted a familiar figure: Brigitte Bouvier. She was standing nearby, admiring a sleek gray colt. She was wearing form-fitting khakis, a beige linen shirt, and riding boots. She had an auction catalog in her hand and was making notes in it.

Frank remembered that Joe had expressed some doubts about the story she'd given to the police. Brigitte had claimed that she hadn't known Marco before last night. Maybe this was an opportunity to see whether or not she had been telling the truth, Frank thought.

He walked up to her. "Good morning," he called out pleasantly. "I hope you've recovered from your ordeal."

Brigitte stopped scribbling in her catalog and smiled at Frank. He noticed that she had dark circles under her eyes. "Good morning, Monsieur Hardy," she murmured. "To tell you the truth, I did not sleep very much. I was having many nightmares about Monsieur Donatelli."

"That's terrible," Frank said sympathetically. "By the way, you can call me Frank."

"All right—Frank." The way she said his name, it sounded like "Frenk."

Frank moved closer to her and lowered his voice. "You know, I heard some rumors that Marco Donatelli wasn't a very nice guy," he fibbed. "I suppose he could have had a lot of enemies."

Brigitte shrugged. "I have no idea. I did not know him personally."

"But you *had* heard of him?" Frank asked her.

"Oh, yes," Brigitte said, brushing a wisp of honey blond hair back from her face. "I used to read about him in a magazine called *Le Scandale*. They had many articles about him because he was—how you say it?—a playboy."

Now, that's interesting, Frank thought. Was it possible that Marco had been killed by a jealous girlfriend or ex-girlfriend? She could have seen him flirting with Brigitte, and possibly others, and worked herself into a murderous rage. He'd have to check around and see if anyone had spotted Marco at the party with a woman.

Brigitte touched Frank's arm and nodded at the gray colt. "Tell me what you think of this little one," she said with a smile. "Should I buy him? Or should I save my money for Goldenrod?"

Frank stared at Brigitte. He had the distinct impression that she was trying to direct the conversation away from Marco's murder and onto a more benign topic. She was being very smooth and subtle about it, too.

So she's smooth and subtle, Frank thought. Why does that make me not trust her?

Joe paused in front of one of the stalls, trying to figure out where to go next. Suddenly he felt something wet and slimy on his cheek.

"What the—" Joe glanced in the stall. Standing there was a reddish brown horse, her nose an inch away from Joe's face.

"Oh, great," Joe muttered. "I've just been kissed by a horse." He frowned at her. "No offense, but I would have enjoyed that a lot more if you'd been five feet six, blond, blue-eyed—you get the picture."

The horse tried to nuzzle Joe's face again. Joe stepped back quickly. "Take it easy, pony. One kiss is my limit, okay?"

Joe noticed a sign hanging over the horse's stall door. It said:

HIP #461
CHESTNUT FILLY
DAM: MAGIC WAND
SIRE: FIRESTORM
PROPERTY OF WHISPERING
HOLLOW FARM

"Dam and sire," Joe said to himself. "Now, let's see. Dam means mother and sire means father. Or is it the other way around?"

"Lovely horse, isn't she?"

Joe turned around. A man with short black hair and a pencil-thin mustache was standing behind him. He appeared to be in his early forties and was dressed in an elegant white suit that set off his dark complexion. Next to him were two beefy guys who were eyeing Joe suspiciously.

Joe recognized the man right away as Prince Zafir of Morocco; Joe had seen him the night before at the party. He knew the prince was in town to make a bid on Goldenrod. He also knew that the two guys with him were his bodyguards.

"Yeah, great horse," Joe replied after a moment. He felt a little uneasy; he wasn't sure how he was supposed to address the prince. Your Excellency? he wondered. Your highness? He definitely wasn't up on his royal etiquette.

In any case, Joe was glad he'd run into the prince. He wanted to ask him some questions about Marco Donatelli.

"Have you seen the famous Goldenrod?" the prince asked Joe. He was soft-spoken, and his English was perfect.

"Um, actually, no," Joe said. "I've been meaning to do that."

"Let us walk together, then," the prince said graciously. "I was on my way there now."

On the way to Goldenrod's stall, the prince talked amiably about a variety of subjects: the auction, local history, American baseball. It took

Joe a few minutes to steer the conversation around to the previous night—and Marco's murder.

"Oh, yes, most unfortunate," the prince murmured, clasping his hands behind his back. "I actually spoke to Mr. Donatelli during the party. And to think that he was dead a short time after . . ." He shook his head sadly.

Joe tried not to look too eager. "You spoke to him, huh? I suppose you talked about race car driving or something?"

"Actually, we talked about Goldenrod, since we both planned to bid on him. Mr. Donatelli was trying to learn how high I was going to go." The prince shrugged. "Of course, I did not reveal that information. One should never tip one's hand to one's enemies, so to speak." His face lit up suddenly. "Ah, there he is. Is he not the most glorious creature you have ever seen?"

Joe looked up. A handler was cantering a yearling around a grassy area. He was small and slender, with a shiny, golden brown coat and long, spindly legs. He moved gracefully, his sinewy muscles rippling.

Joe didn't know one thing about horses, but he felt an instinctive thrill of excitement as he looked at Goldenrod. It wasn't just that he was beautiful. He was also famous: the one and only foal of the legendary Golden Folly.

A middle-aged man who was watching Goldenrod turned around. He was tall and muscular, and his auburn hair was streaked with gray. He was wearing a ten-gallon hat, jeans, a denim shirt, and red lizard cowboy boots.

"Howdy, Prince," the man said to Prince Zafir, tipping his hat. "I see you've come to check out my horse." He spoke with a heavy Texas drawl.

Prince Zafir laughed. "*Your* horse, Mr. Vaughn? You sound very sure of yourself."

"Oh, I am," Mr. Vaughn replied, grinning confidently. "I don't intend to leave the auction tomorrow without Goldenrod."

At that moment, Mr. Vaughn noticed Joe. "Don't tell me you've got designs on Goldenrod, too, young man?" he boomed cheerfully.

"Oh, no," Joe said quickly. "I just spent my last million, so I won't be buying any horses tomorrow."

Mr. Vaughn chuckled and slapped Joe's back hard. "You're funny. My daughter'd like you. Hey, Chelsea!" he called out suddenly. "Hey, hon? Someone here I want you to meet!"

A girl who was talking to one of the handlers glanced over. Joe couldn't believe it. It was the girl from the party—the one who'd bumped into him at the buffet table!

She spotted Joe, and her brown eyes widened. Then she walked over and stood next to her father. She didn't look terribly thrilled.

"This is my little girl, Chelsea," Mr. Vaughn

told Joe. "I'm sorry, son, but I didn't catch your name."

"Joe Hardy," Joe mumbled.

Mr. Vaughn slapped Joe on the back again. "Joe Hardy. Pleased to meet you. By the way, my name's Vaughn—Wyatt Vaughn." He added, "Why don't you two young people talk? The prince and I have some horse business to discuss."

Mr. Vaughn turned to Prince Zafir, leaving Joe with Chelsea.

"Um, hi," Joe said, feeling incredibly awkward.

"Hi." Chelsea stuffed her hands into the pockets of her jeans and looked at the ground.

Joe stared at her for a moment. He thought she looked really cute with her long auburn hair pulled back in a ponytail. "Listen. Maybe we got off to the wrong start last night," he said. "I'm sorry about what happened."

Chelsea's mouth curled up in a hint of a smile. "Um, I'm sorry, too. I guess I was in kind of a bad mood."

"Tough day?" Joe asked her.

"No. I don't like parties much, that's all. You know, meeting total strangers, making stupid small talk, stuff like that." Chelsea turned and grinned affectionately at Goldenrod. Then she looked at Joe. "I'd much rather spend my time riding."

"So what I hear you saying is that you're a horse person, not a people person," Joe said.

"Yeah, I guess. That's why Daddy wanted to introduce you to me. He's always trying to force new friends on me." Chelsea quickly put her hand to her mouth. "Oops! That came out real bad, didn't it? I didn't mean that I minded being introduced to you. In fact, I'm kind of glad."

Joe smiled at her. "I'm glad, too."

Their eyes locked for a moment, and a brief silence fell between them. Joe cleared his throat, then said, "So you really like Goldenrod, huh?"

Chelsea beamed. "Oh, yes. I think he's the most beautiful horse I've ever seen. And he has a real sweet personality, too."

"Well, I hope you and your dad get him at tomorrow's auction, then," Joe told her.

"I don't know," Chelsea said uncertainly. She glanced over at her father, who was kneeling beside Goldenrod's back legs and inspecting her shins. He was chatting with Prince Zafir, who was standing nearby. "It all depends on whether my daddy can outbid the others," Chelsea went on. "Lots of people want her, you know. Like the prince, and that actor Luke Ventura, and that woman from Paris. Marco Donatelli wanted him, too."

"Yeah, but your dad seems pretty determined—"

Joe's words were cut off by the sound of frantic whinnying. In a flash, Goldenrod kicked his rear legs up, knocking Mr. Vaughn to the ground. Mr. Vaughn grunted, then his eyelids fluttered shut.

"Daddy!" Chelsea screamed.

Joe saw that Mr. Vaughn was unconscious. He also saw that Goldenrod was continuing to kick wildly. With each motion, his back hooves were landing closer and closer to Mr. Vaughn's head. In seconds the Texan would be trampled!

Joe shot into action. With lightning speed, he dove to the ground and grabbed Mr. Vaughn. But before he could roll himself and Mr. Vaughn out of harm's way, he saw a sharp hoof come down just inches away from his face. Now *he* was about to be trampled!

Chapter
Eight

THIS IS NOT a good place to be, Joe thought.

Out of the corner of his eye Joe saw Goldenrod kick his back legs up. This was his opportunity. In the split second before the yearling's legs came down again, Joe tightened his hold on Mr. Vaughn and rolled several feet away. Goldenrod's back hooves landed heavily on the ground, stirring up a cloud of dust and grass.

Joe took a deep breath. He and Mr. Vaughn were safe for the moment. Joe leapt to his feet, then dragged Mr. Vaughn out of Goldenrod's range. He glanced around quickly and spotted Chelsea.

"Get a doctor," he called out breathlessly. Chelsea nodded mutely, then took off.

At the same time, Goldenrod's handler came

running up and attempted to subdue him. Joe also saw Eileen's brother Sean rushing over. Seeing that Goldenrod was being taken care of, Joe returned his attention to Mr. Vaughn. He was beginning to regain consciousness; his eyes were half open, and he was groaning.

"Mr. Vaughn?" Joe said loudly. "Mr. Vaughn, can you hear me?"

"Is that you, John Hardy?" Mr. Vaughn muttered, touching his forehead gingerly. "W-what happened?"

"It's *Joe* Hardy, Mr. Vaughn," Joe corrected him. "You got kicked by Goldenrod. But hang on—your daughter's gone to get a doctor for you."

Prince Zafir leaned over Mr. Vaughn, his eyes full of concern. "Is he all right?" he asked Joe.

"He's conscious, anyway," Joe replied.

One of the prince's bodyguards started saying something to the prince in rapid-fire Arabic. The other one was pointing toward the parking lot. The prince frowned and shook his head. Joe didn't understand the exchange, but it seemed as though the bodyguards were trying to get the prince away from the scene.

Chelsea came rushing up with a young, dark-haired guy. "This is Dr. Rappaport," she told Joe. Then she glanced at her father and let out a squeal of delight. "Oh, Daddy, you're okay! Oh, I'm so glad!" She knelt down beside him and gave him a big kiss on the cheek. "I brought you a doctor, Daddy. You'd better let him examine you."

Joe stood up to make room for the doctor. He noticed that Goldenrod was considerably calmer, although he was panting slightly. Sean was examining his left flank. A paunchy, middle-aged man with thinning brown hair was standing by Sean's side, a shell-shocked expression on his face. Joe recognized him as Goldenrod's owner, Abe Addison.

"So what's the verdict?" Joe asked Sean. "Why did Goldenrod lose it like that?"

Sean held up a pair of tweezers. Pinched between them was a small dart. "This," he said gravely.

As Joe leaned over to examine the dart, he caught a familiar odor: bitter almonds. "Cyanide?" Joe said incredulously. "Someone tried to kill Goldenrod with a cyanide-laced dart?"

Abe Addison grabbed Sean's arm. "Tell it to me straight, Doc," he said urgently. "Is he going to make it?"

"It's an excellent sign that he isn't displaying any of the usual cyanide poisoning symptoms, Abe," Sean replied. "My guess is that the dose was too small." Pulling out his cellular phone, he added, "In any case, I want to call my assistant and ask her to bring me an antidote. She should be here within a few minutes." He began dialing.

"That's good news—I suppose," Mr. Addison said uncertainly. He reached into the pocket of his jacket, got out a bottle of pills, and popped one into his mouth. "My ulcer's killing me," he muttered to no one in particular.

Joe glanced around. There was a crowd of onlookers standing around, gaping at the scene, and talking excitedly. He didn't see Oliver Fairfield, though. "I'd better find Mr. Fairfield so he can call the police," he told Sean and Mr. Addison.

As he walked toward the Fairfield, Inc., building, Joe scanned the area nervously. He realized that a sniper had taken a shot at Goldenrod from somewhere nearby. He had no doubt that the person was long gone; too much time had passed, and it would have been easy enough to melt into the crowd or slip out of one of the side entrances and onto the street.

Who could have wanted Goldenrod dead? he wondered. Certainly, lots of people wanted him alive. But what possible motive could anyone have for killing him?

"What's a quinella?" George asked.

She had her face buried in the program for that day's races. It was almost one o'clock, and she and Nancy were walking through the front gates of the Saratoga Racetrack.

"It's a bet," Nancy explained. "You pick two horses that you think will come in first and second. But it doesn't matter which one comes in first and which one comes in second—you win money either way." She added, "But remember—we're not here to bet on horses. We're here to find Popeye Lopez."

George looked up from the program and glanced around. "I hope we can. This place is a zoo. It sure wasn't like this when we had breakfast here yesterday!"

George was right, Nancy thought. The grassy area between the front gates and the grandstand was mobbed with hundreds of people. Many of them were sitting on lawn chairs or under green-and white-striped tents, and they studied their programs intently, trying to figure out which horses to bet on. There were booths with hot dogs, soft drinks, souvenirs, and T-shirts for sale. Closed-circuit television sets were mounted every fifty feet or so, showing the action on the track.

A voice came over the loudspeaker. "Ladies and gentlemen. In the first race, Number Four and Number Six are scratches. I repeat, Four and Six are scratches. The race will begin in approximately fifteen minutes."

"Misty Meadow and Ain't Misbehavin' are scratches?" Nancy heard a woman say in a disappointed tone. "I was going to bet on those horses!"

On the way to the grandstand, Nancy and George saw the horses for the first race being trotted to the track by their jockeys. They moved along a roped-off path adjacent to the back of the grandstand. Nancy marveled at the beauty of the horses, at their smooth, muscled bodies and gleaming coats. She also noticed that the jockeys were all wearing bright, festive colors: hot pink, lime green, neon yellow, and tangerine orange.

After watching the horses for a moment, Nancy and George proceeded to the grandstand. Nancy had read in one of her guidebooks that the grandstand dated from 1902. A long, elegant building with high, sloping roofs, it overlooked an enormous oval dirt track. Inside that track was a secondary track made of grass. And at the very center was a large, old-fashioned-looking sign with information about the first race: what horses were in the race, their odds, and how many dollars had been bet on them as of that minute.

Nancy and George found their seats, which were near the finish line. Their plan was to watch the first race, then wander around the premises in search of Popeye.

"These seats are great," George said. "How did we get them?"

"My dad has a good friend who lives in Saratoga," Nancy explained.

She noticed that the people sitting around them were all dressed to the hilt. A lot of the women were wearing pastel-colored dresses and large matching hats. Many of the men wore white linen suits and bow ties. Nancy felt a little out of place in her denim skirt and pink T-shirt.

A few rows down, a TV reporter was interviewing a middle-aged man. Nancy recognized him as the governor of New York.

Then Nancy turned toward the track. The jockeys were trotting their horses out to the starting gate. She remembered Jimmy on Wednesday morning, staring pensively at the thoroughbreds and not paying a bit of attention to the conversation around him. Where was he now? she wondered. Was he okay?

Frank paused at the railing near the starting gate and wiped the sweat off his brow. The August sun was beating down, and there was no shade in that particular spot.

He and Joe had come to the races with Mr. Fairfield and his guests: Brigitte Bouvier, Prince Zafir and his pair of bodyguards, Luke Ventura, and several others. But Frank had left Mr. Fairfield's private box to take a closer look at the track.

Mr. Fairfield's expedition had almost been canceled because of Marco's murder and the attack on Goldenrod that morning. But Goldenrod had pulled through, thanks to Sean's speedy treatment. And everyone had been eager for a distraction from the grim adventures of the last two days. As for Mr. Vaughn, he was back in his hotel room recovering from the blow to his head.

Frank wondered if the yearling had been the target of the poisoned dart or whether someone standing near the horse, possibly Mr. Vaughn, was the target. And if so, was the incident connected to Marco's murder? Was there a killer on the loose, and was he or she targeting various people who would be attending the yearling auction the next day?

Frank was distracted from his thoughts by the sound of a bugle call. The first race was about to begin. The horses were all in the starting gate; the jockeys were bent low in their saddles, focused and ready to go.

A gun sounded, the gates burst open, and the horses exploded out. "And they're off!" the voice over the loudspeaker cried.

The horses took off like lightning, leaving a cloud of dust in their wake. Frank watched, mesmerized. The colors of the jockeys' jerseys flashed past him in a blur.

"Canterbury Tales takes an early lead, with KeepOnTruckinMama close behind," the announcer said. "Belle of the Ball is in third place along with Doctor Doom, and Cyberhorse is in fourth place."

Craning his neck to see over the people in front of him, Frank followed the horses as they rounded the first curve. It was hard to see which horse was where, but the announcer's constant updates helped.

In a moment, the horses came thundering down the final stretch. KeepOnTruckinMama was in first place, but Doctor Doom was catching up fast. The crowd was at a fever pitch of excitement; the people around Frank were jumping up and down and screaming.

At the last second, Doctor Doom passed KeepOnTruckinMama and crossed the finish line. "And it's Doctor Doom by half a length, followed by KeepOnTruckinMama and Girl Friday!" the announcer shouted.

Frank peered at his watch. The race had taken almost no time at all. Amazing, he thought.

Glancing up at the grandstand seats behind him, he decided to head back to Mr. Fairfield's box. But just then a familiar figure caught his eye. Brigitte Bouvier was weaving through the crowd in front of the grandstand. She wore a hat and sunglasses to shield her face from the sun, and she was clutching her purse tightly to her chest.

Curious, Frank decided to follow her. She was way ahead of him, but he managed to keep her in sight, nevertheless. Brigitte reached the far end of the grandstand and turned the corner, out of Frank's view. Frank sped up; he didn't want to lose her.

A few minutes later, Frank reached the far end of the grandstand. He turned the corner and stopped in confusion. Before him was a grassy, deserted area enclosed by the east wall of the grandstand and several small maintenance buildings. Brigitte was nowhere in sight.

"Brigitte?" Frank called out. There was no reply.

Where could she have gone? Frank wondered. The area was clearly not meant for anyone but the track's employees. Just then he heard a loud groaning noise from behind one of the buildings.

He rushed to the source of the noise. He couldn't believe his eyes.

Brigitte was lying on the ground. Her clothes were disheveled, and her face was ghostly white.

Chapter
Nine

FRANK KNELT DOWN beside Brigitte. She shrank away from him. "N-no . . ." she moaned weakly.

"It's okay," Frank said quickly, taking her hand in his. "It's me, Frank Hardy."

Brigitte stared at him groggily. "Monsieur Hardy—I mean, Frank. I am so glad it is you. Someone—someone tried to kill me."

"What!" Frank exclaimed.

His eyes swept over her, checking for injuries. He didn't see any. However, he did notice something lying on the ground near her head: a crumpled handkerchief.

He picked it up and held it up to his nose. Just as he thought: chloroform.

"What happened, Brigitte?" he asked her grimly.

Brigitte tried to sit up slightly, then gasped at the effort and lay back down. "I was taking a walk," she began. "All these people . . . I wanted to find a quiet place. So I came here. But I heard footsteps, and someone grabbed me. They put a cloth over my nose."

"Do you know if it was a man or a woman?" Frank asked.

"I think it was a man, although I am not positive," Brigitte replied. "But then someone— it must have been you—called out my name. And the man let me go and ran away."

Frank nodded. He glanced around; the area was still deserted. He had to get a doctor and the police, but he didn't want to leave Brigitte there, in case her attacker doubled back.

He bent down and put his arm under Brigitte's shoulders. "I'm going to carry you out of here," he told her. "Do you think you can make it?"

"I think so," Brigitte murmured. She closed her eyes as Frank scooped her up in his arms and stood up. "I feel very sleepy. Why am I so sleepy?"

"It's a drug," Frank replied. "Don't worry. You're going to be all right."

As soon as Frank arrived at the main part of the grandstand, he spotted a security guard. He called the guard over and explained what had happened.

"I'll get the house medic and the police,"

the guard said immediately. He took a cellular phone out of his pocket and began speaking into it.

"And while you're at it, could you page Joe Hardy and ask him to get here immediately?" Frank asked him.

While the guard made his calls, Frank studied Brigitte's face. Her eyes were closed, and her cheeks were pale. Who had done this to her? he wondered. Was it the same person who'd killed Marco Donatelli? And was that person responsible for the poisoned dart?

What on earth was going on?

"Joe Hardy, please come to Grandstand Area Z. Joe Hardy, Grandstand Area Z."

Nancy stopped and glanced up at the loudspeaker. She and George were walking out of one of the grandstand restaurants. They were making a round of all the racetrack's eateries, inquiring about Popeye. "I wonder who's paging Joe?" she asked George.

George shrugged. "Who knows? Maybe Frank."

Nancy's blue eyes lit up. She grabbed George's arm. "Hey, this gives me an idea. I know how we can find Popeye!"

"How?" George asked her.

"We'll page him!" Nancy said excitedly. "If he's here today, maybe he'll show up."

The two friends walked over to the Information Booth and arranged for the page. A few minutes later, a voice came over the loudspeaker:

"Popeye Lopez, please report to the Information Booth. There is an important message for you. Popeye Lopez, Information Booth."

"Perfect," Nancy said. She leaned against the booth and glanced at her watch. "Now we just wait for him to identify himself."

As Nancy waited for Popeye to show up, she thought about the events of the last twenty-four hours. First there was Marco Donatelli's murder; then there was the knife and note that someone had left for her in her hotel room. Finally, there was the threatening phone call afterward.

Nancy had called Eileen that morning to see if Jimmy had been acquainted with Marco Donatelli. Eileen had said she wasn't sure. Nancy had also called Noah several times, to try and get his story on his whereabouts the night before. But each time she called, she reached his answering machine. On the way to the track, she and George had stopped by his apartment; either he wasn't there, or he wasn't answering the door.

"The second race will begin in approximately ten minutes," the announcer's voice boomed over the loudspeaker. "Please note that Number Five is a scratch."

Hordes of people passed the Information Booth on their way to the betting windows. Nancy watched them as she waited for Popeye to show up. Then she noticed someone coming toward them: Eileen's brother Sean. He smiled cheerfully at Nancy and waved.

"Small world," he called out. "Are you enjoying this crazy place? Overloading on the smell of hot dogs and buttered popcorn?"

"Actually, we're here on business," Nancy explained. She turned to George. "This is Eileen's brother Sean. Sean, this is my friend George. I don't think you two met at the party last night."

Sean shook George's hand. "It's a pleasure," he said. "So you guys are here on business, huh? Sounds serious."

Nancy told him that they were looking for Popeye Lopez to try to get some information on his alleged conversations with Jimmy. "Eileen says there's no way Jimmy could have a gambling problem," she finished. "I want to talk to Popeye and see what he has to say."

Suddenly Sean looked uncomfortable. Nancy remembered seeing a similar expression on his face the night before, when Eileen had told him about Jimmy's supposed gambling problem and the theft of the *Sentinel*'s petty cash.

Nancy touched his arm. "Sean? Is there something you're hiding about Jimmy?"

Sean was silent for a moment. "I'll tell you two because I think it's important that you know," he said finally. "But please don't say a word to Eileen. It would really devastate her."

Nancy and George exchanged a glance. "Go on," Nancy said, curious.

"I've been at the track pretty often since the season started," Sean began. "I look after some of the horses. Anyway, I've seen Jimmy here twice. Both times he was at the fifty-dollar betting window."

"The fifty-dollar betting window?" George repeated. "What's that?"

"It's where you place bets of fifty dollars or more," Sean explained. "The second time I was here, I went up to Jimmy to see what the deal was. Right away he asked me if I could lend him a hundred dollars. When I told him no, that I didn't have that kind of cash on me, he got angry and stormed off."

"You're kidding!" George exclaimed.

Sean shrugged sadly. "I wish I were. I didn't have the heart to tell Eileen about the incident, so I didn't. Just between you and me, I wasn't surprised to hear that he'd disappeared and that cash was missing from the *Sentinel* office. And to tell you the truth, I'm kind of glad he's gone. My sister deserves better."

Nancy was silent as she digested what Sean was saying. She still couldn't imagine Jimmy being a gambler, but there was no denying Sean's story. On the other hand, even if Jimmy was a gambler, it didn't mean he was a thief, too. It also didn't mean that she should stop looking for him.

Just then something caught her eye. A short, bald, beefy guy was standing behind a nearby column, watching her, George, and Sean. He was dressed in a neon blue windbreaker, white T-shirt, and tan slacks. As soon as he saw that Nancy had spotted him, he turned and walked very fast in the opposite direction.

Maybe that's Popeye! Nancy thought. She turned to George and Sean. "Um, excuse me, okay? I'll be right back."

"But, Nancy—" George began.

"I'll explain later," Nancy said quickly. "Wait for me here."

Nancy took off running. The guy glanced over his shoulder, saw that Nancy was after him, and started running, too. Nancy had a hard time following him. There were way too many people, especially now that the second race was about to begin.

Finally, she reached a corridor leading to the restrooms. She thought she'd seen the guy heading this way, but now she wasn't sure. He was nowhere to be seen.

Frustrated, Nancy glanced around. "Now what?" she said to herself.

Suddenly she felt something hard jab her in the ribs. "Don't make a sound," a low, gruff voice whispered in her ear. "I've got a gun in my pocket, and if you make a move, I'll shoot you right through the heart!"

Chapter
Ten

Nancy stiffened with fear. Don't panic, she told herself. There are lots of people around. This guy won't shoot you in a public place.

Turning her head ever so slightly, she managed to catch a peek at her assailant. She wasn't surprised to see that it was the guy she'd been chasing.

"You're Popeye Lopez, aren't you?" she asked.

"Think you're pretty smart, don't you?" Popeye growled. He put his hand on her elbow and continued to jam the point of his gun into her ribs. "Come with me. We're going to have a little talk. And don't even think about calling out for help."

As Popeye led her out of the grandstand toward the parking lot, Nancy considered trying to make her escape. She didn't think Popeye would carry out his threat and shoot her. But on the other hand, why take a chance?

They soon reached a fairly secluded area at the edge of the parking lot. There were no people nearby, but Nancy could see that the spot was visible from a concession stand a hundred feet away.

Nancy stopped in her tracks and faced Popeye. "This is far enough," she told the man firmly.

Popeye stared at her, surprised. Then he narrowed his beady black eyes and sneered at her. "I don't take orders from girls," Popeye growled. "But this spot's as good as any, I suppose."

Nancy glanced at the right bottom pocket of his windbreaker. Now she wondered whether he had a gun at all or whether he'd been faking it. "You don't really have a gun in there, do you?" she demanded.

Popeye took a menacing step toward her. "Shut up!" he snarled. "*I* ask the questions. And here's a real simple one. Why have you been looking for me?"

The waiter at the Palomino Grill must have told him, Nancy thought.

"Some people have seen you with Jimmy English recently," Nancy said. "I want to know what you were talking about."

"What for?" Popeye asked her suspiciously.

"Jimmy's disappeared," Nancy explained. "And—"

But before she could go on, Popeye cut her off. "Jimmy's . . . disappeared?" he repeated. He'd turned white as a sheet.

Nancy was startled by Popeye's reaction. "Yes, he's disappeared. He was last seen Wednesday night."

Popeye glanced around nervously. "What are you saying? That he was kidnapped or something?"

"We don't know," Nancy told him. Then she explained about the missing petty cash as well as Tracy Kim's idea that Jimmy had gambling debts. *"Did* Jimmy owe money?" she asked Popeye. "Is that what the two of you were talking about?"

Popeye looked incredulous. "Jimmy English a gambler? Who came up with a crazy idea like that? The kid's a straight arrow through and through."

"Then what were the two of you discussing?" Nancy persisted. It was clear that Popeye knew *something* about Jimmy. Otherwise, he wouldn't have reacted so strangely to the news of his disappearance.

"I gotta split," Popeye said suddenly.

"But I need your help," Nancy said.

Popeye turned and strode toward the parking lot. "Stay away from me," he called over his shoulder. "And don't tell *anyone* you talked to me."

Nancy stood there and watched him go. She thought about running after him, but then changed her mind. There was no way she could make him talk if he didn't want to.

Popeye was definitely afraid, she thought. But of what? Or whom? And just what did he know about Jimmy's disappearance?

Frank watched as Brigitte was led into a taxi by the Saratoga Raceway doctor. The doctor was going to accompany her to the hospital so she could have a more thorough examination.

Frank turned to Joe. The two of them were standing in a special service driveway in back of the raceway. With Brigitte and the doctor leaving, the Hardys were alone. Off in the distance, Frank could hear the sounds of the second race starting.

"Let's try to figure this thing out," Frank said tensely. "For starters, what do Marco Donatelli, Goldenrod, and Brigitte Bouvier have in common?"

"Are you thinking that the same person went after all three of them?" Joe asked his brother.

"I think it's a safe assumption," Frank replied. "The question is motive. Why try to do away with two people and a horse? That is, unless Goldenrod wasn't the target at all, and the assailant was really aiming at Mr. Vaughn."

"That makes more sense," Joe agreed.

Frank looked thoughtful. "Okay, so say that the assailant was after Marco, Brigitte, and Mr. Vaughn. Then we're looking at—"

"Three of the five people who plan to bid on Goldenrod tomorrow," Joe finished. "The other two being Prince Zafir and Luke Ventura."

"Now we're getting somewhere," Frank said, his brown eyes flashing. "So let's consider the possibilities. One, our assailant is someone we don't know, and he or she is after all of Goldenrod's potential bidders for some reason. Two, our assailant is either Prince Zafir or Luke Ventura, who wants Goldenrod so much that he's willing to eliminate the competition—literally. Three—"

"I just thought of something," Joe said suddenly. "The prince left his seat right after Brigitte did. As soon as the first race was over, Brigitte told me that she was going to take a walk and get some fresh air. About a minute later, the prince got up and left the box. His bodyguards tried to follow him, but he wouldn't let them."

"Did anyone else leave their seats?" Frank asked.

Joe shook his head. "Nope, not that I noticed."

Frank grabbed Joe's arm. "Come on, let's get back to our seats. I want to talk to Prince Zafir right away. I hope he's come back."

But when they got to Mr. Fairfield's private box, Prince Zafir and his bodyguards were nowhere to be seen. Mr. Fairfield was talking to Luke Ventura and his other guests about the second race, which had just concluded. The box was large and luxurious with a dozen seats overlooking the final stretch. On a small table there were pitchers of iced tea and platters of sandwiches and fresh fruit. Down below, the winner of the second race, Mogul Mania, was getting his picture taken in the Winner's Circle along with his jockey, trainer, and owner.

Frank managed to get Mr. Fairfield away from the others and told him about the attack on Brigitte.

"Is Ms. Bouvier all right?" Mr. Fairfield demanded when Frank had finished. "Where is she? Has a doctor seen her?"

"The raceway doctor took her to the hospital to check her out," Joe explained. "He said she looked fine, but he wanted to make sure."

"We think this attack might be linked to Marco Donatelli's murder and the poisoned dart incident," Frank went on. "In any case, we need to ask Prince Zafir some questions. Is he around?"

Mr. Fairfield looked startled. "The prince? Why would you want to question him?"

"Just some routine stuff," Joe replied casually. "Don't worry, sir, we'll be very diplomatic."

"I don't know," Mr. Fairfield said doubtfully. "Anyway, he's gone. He and his men left about twenty minutes ago. The prince said he wanted to go home and rest before the polo match this evening."

"Where is he staying?" Frank asked him.

Mr. Fairfield glanced around nervously. "He's renting the Mulligan mansion out by Saratoga Lake," he said in a low voice. "But that information is for your ears only. The prince is extremely careful about his privacy."

The Mulligan mansion was an ornate Victorian house on the outskirts of Saratoga. Nestled in a grove of pine trees and overlooking Saratoga Lake, it was nearly invisible from the road.

As Frank pulled up the long driveway that curved to the front of the house, Joe whistled. "Pretty fancy digs," he murmured appreciatively. "It sure beats our little room at the motel."

Frank had to agree. The house was twice as big as Oliver Fairfield's and had beautiful architectural details: a gabled roof, several stone chimneys, and stained glass windows. Out back, he could make out a swimming pool, two tennis courts, and an enormous cedar hot tub.

There was a silver Jaguar in the driveway as well as a small red sports car. "Looks like they're home," Joe observed, stepping out of the van.

Frank and Joe went up to the front door and knocked. No one answered. "That's weird," Frank muttered, then knocked again.

After what seemed like an eternity, the door

opened, and one of the prince's bodyguards peered out. He frowned when he saw the Hardys but said nothing.

"Hey, there," Joe said cheerfully. "Is the prince home? We'd like to have a chat with him."

The bodyguard glowered and began closing the door. Joe stuck his foot in the opening. "Not so fast. We'd like to speak to the prince—now."

"It's a business matter," Frank explained quickly. "We work for Mr. Fairfield—"

But before he could get any further, the bodyguard opened the door and stepped outside. The other bodyguard materialized behind him. His eyes were cold and hard.

"Are you getting the feeling that we're not welcome here?" Joe asked Frank uneasily.

Frank didn't have a chance to reply. The first bodyguard said something to the other in Arabic, and the two reached into their pockets. Before Frank knew what was happening, they were brandishing knives—and coming toward him and Joe!

Chapter
Eleven

EYEING THE KNIVES warily, Frank took a step back and raised his hands in the air. He smiled nervously at the bodyguards. "You've got this all wrong. We're not here to hurt the prince. We just want to talk to him."

But the bodyguards were either unable or unwilling to comprehend Frank's words. They said something to each other, then one of them came charging toward Frank, making slicing motions in the air with his knife. The other went after Joe.

Realizing that the time for polite talk was over, Frank went into action. He intercepted his assailant's knife arm, then delivered a grueling kick to the man's abdomen. The bodyguard grunted and doubled over. Then Frank pinned the man's knife arm in back of him and squeezed his wrist in a powerful viselike grip. The bodyguard yelped in pain, his fingers fluttered open, and the knife fell to the ground. Frank bent down and picked it up.

In the meantime, the other bodyguard, who was the larger of the two, was wrestling on the ground with Joe. The man was on top of Joe, and the two were fighting for the knife. The tip of the knife trembled over Joe's throat.

Frank was about to come to his brother's rescue, but at the last minute, Joe let out a loud growl, arched his back, and pushed the bodyguard off. The bodyguard yelled out in surprise and landed on the ground in a thud. Joe leapt to his feet, breathing heavily. He was about to make another move when the bodyguard unexpectedly thrust his legs out and scissored them around Joe's ankles. Joe went flying to the ground.

"What is going on here?"

Frank whirled around. Prince Zafir was standing in the doorway of the house. He was dressed in a gray silk robe, and the expression on his face was anything but happy.

The bodyguard who'd gone after Frank said something to the prince in Arabic. The other bodyguard jumped to his feet. Joe stood up and brushed the dirt off his khakis.

The prince raised his hands in the air, silencing the bodyguards. "My men tell me that you were trying to break into the house," he said quietly to the Hardys.

"You're joking, right?" Joe snapped.

"That's not what happened," Frank said calmly. "We're part of Mr. Fairfield's security staff. We came here to ask you some questions, and your bodyguards wouldn't let us through the door. Instead, they came after us with knives."

The prince frowned, then said a few words to his bodyguards. After a moment, he turned back to the Hardys. "I must apologize most sincerely for their behavior," he said. "They were only trying to protect me, and they did not understand you. You see, they do not speak English. I trust that neither of you was hurt. Why don't you come inside, and we can talk there?"

Without waiting for a reply, the prince went into the house. Frank and Joe exchanged a glance, then followed him. The bodyguards followed as well, glaring with hostility at the Hardys the whole time.

The prince led the brothers into a large sitting room. Frank noted that it was decorated with priceless antiques and oriental rugs.

The prince sat down in a Louis XIV chair and gestured for Frank and Joe to take the couch across from him. "Please," he said. "Now, what did you come here to see me about?"

Frank sat down on the couch and tried to collect his thoughts. He wanted to form his words carefully. It would not be a smart move to offend the prince of Morocco, even if he *was* a suspect in the case.

"I don't know if you've heard, but Brigitte Bouvier was attacked by someone at the race-track," Frank said finally. "She went for a walk between the first and second races and wandered into a deserted area. Someone grabbed her from behind and tried to chloroform her."

The prince lifted his eyebrows. He looked genuinely concerned. "Is Ms. Bouvier all right?"

"She's at the hospital getting checked out, but she seems to be okay," Joe said. "The thing is, I saw you leave your seat at about the time she did—"

"And we were wondering if you might have seen anyone following her," Frank finished quickly. He didn't want the prince to think that he and Joe suspected him.

"Me? No." The prince leaned forward and picked up a small vase of orchids from the coffee table. He ran a finger over one of the orchids, then put the vase back down again. "I saw someone I recognized in another box, and I went over to talk to him," he continued. "I have no idea where Ms. Bouvier went or if anyone was following her."

The phone rang just then. One of the body-guards answered it. After a minute, he handed the cordless phone to the prince and muttered something in Arabic.

The prince took the phone and cupped his hand over the mouthpiece. "An overseas call I have been expecting," he explained, smiling at the Hardys. "Could we continue this conversation later—perhaps at the polo match? Mr. Fairfield asked us all to join him there at six, correct?"

"That's right," Frank said, standing up. "Thank you for your time. We'll see you at the match."

The bodyguards, who'd been hovering by the door, moved to lead Frank and Joe out. "We can see ourselves out," Joe told them pointedly. The bodyguards scowled at him.

Once outside, Frank turned to Joe. "Well, what did you think?"

"I think I'd like to challenge those two jerks to a rematch," Joe said angrily.

Frank frowned in exasperation. "No, I meant about the prince. Did you think he was on the level about Brigitte?"

"He seemed to be, but it was hard to tell for sure," Joe replied. "And since we can't exactly give him the third degree, it's kind of a problem getting the truth out of him."

Frank pulled the keys to their van out of his pocket. "There's still the polo match tonight," he said with determination. "We'll try him again there—plus talk to Luke Ventura, too. One way or another, we're going to get some answers about Marco's murder and all the other stuff that's been happening."

Nancy and George got back to their hotel shortly after four. After ordering iced coffee, pastries, and fresh fruit from room service, Nancy lay down on the bed. It feels good to be horizontal, she thought.

George set her shoulder bag down on the dresser, kicked off her shoes, and had just sat down on a red velvet chair near the window when the phone rang.

"Just when I was getting comfortable," George said with a sigh. She got up and reached for the phone. "Hello?"

Nancy wondered if the caller might be Noah. She had been leaving messages on his machine all day long. She really wanted to ask him why he'd left the party without them the night before. At the same time, she was a little nervous about talking to him. There was a chance that he'd broken into their hotel room, threatened her life on the phone, and been involved in Jimmy's disappearance and possibly Marco Donatelli's murder, too.

George listened to the caller for a moment, then broke into a radiant smile. "Oh, hi," she said happily. "How are *you?*"

Nancy glanced at her, puzzled. Who could it be? she wondered. It didn't seem as if it was Noah.

George spoke to the person for a few minutes, then covered the mouthpiece with her hand. "It's Luke Ventura," she whispered excitedly to Nancy. "He wants to know if I can go to the Saratoga Performing Arts Center with him tonight. I know we're already going with Eileen. Could I ask him to join us?"

Nancy gave her a thumbs-up sign. "Absolutely," she said enthusiastically.

George said a few more words to Luke, then hung up. "Can you believe it?" she said to Nancy. "A famous movie star asked me out! Me, George Fayne!"

"Well, obviously, Mr. Famous Movie Star has great taste," Nancy told her. Then a thought crossed her mind. "Hey, George? How did he know where you were staying?"

"Oh, I don't know," George said distractedly. "I probably mentioned it to him at Mr. Fairfield's party last night." She walked over to the closet and pulled out a pair of shorts and a T-shirt. "I think I'll try to get a jog in before we get ready to go out. I feel all keyed up."

"We've got food coming up from room service," Nancy reminded her.

There was a knock on the door. "That's probably it now," Nancy said, getting up to answer it.

She looked through the peephole. All she could see was a huge bouquet of red roses. Leaving the chain lock on, Nancy carefully opened the door a crack. The roses shifted slightly, revealing Noah's grinning face.

Nancy's mouth dropped open. "Noah!" She quickly closed the door, unhooked the chain lock, then opened the door again.

Noah stepped through the door and held a finger up to Nancy's lips. "Don't say another word," he said quickly. "I know you're furious with me. I left you at the party without telling you where I was going, and you've tried to call me a million times since then. What can I say? I'm a complete and total jerk."

Before Nancy could reply, Noah got down on his knees before her and handed her the roses. "I hope you'll forgive me," he murmured, "even though I don't deserve it."

Nancy was speechless. Noah had taken her totally by surprise.

George was heading into the bathroom. "I'm going to change for my run," she announced. "Just yell if you need me."

Nancy took the roses from Noah. "Um, thank you for these," she said finally. "They're beautiful."

Noah stood up. "Not nearly as beautiful as you," he said softly.

Nancy turned away. Her mind was racing. She wanted to question Noah, but she knew she had to tread carefully. If he was guilty, he was a potentially dangerous man.

She forced herself to face him and fixed her eyes on his. "Listen, Noah," she said. "We were really confused when you took off from the party without telling any of us. Where did you go?"

"My excuse is very boring," Noah said with a smile. "I got sick. Maybe it was something I ate, or a flu bug—I don't know. Anyway, it came on suddenly, and I just wanted to go home and get into bed. I tried to find you or George or Eileen, but I couldn't. So I left." He added, "I just started feeling okay again a few hours ago. I was going to call you, but then I thought, why not do it in person? So there you have it."

"Did you leave your dad's party before or after Marco Donatelli was murdered?" Nancy asked him levelly.

"Before, I assume," Noah replied. "Marco was on the dance floor with some woman when I left."

Nancy stared at him in silence. Was he telling the truth? she wondered. He sounded sincere, yet there was something about him she just didn't trust. On the other hand, she had to admit that he did look pale and tired, as though he were recovering from an illness.

Noah put his hands on Nancy's shoulders, distracting her from her thoughts. "Listen, let me make it up to you. There's a concert at SPAC tonight. We can sit on the lawn and have a picnic, listen to music, gaze at the stars—"

George emerged from the bathroom, dressed

in shorts and a T-shirt. She glanced at Nancy, then at Noah, then at Nancy again.

"Actually, George and I already have plans to go there with Eileen and Luke Ventura," Nancy told Noah.

"Great," Noah said enthusiastically. "I'll bring a picnic dinner for five, then. I hope you like pasta salad. I'm famous for my pasta salad."

Nancy thought for a moment while Noah stood eagerly in the doorway. Maybe this will be an opportunity to question him some more, she told herself. And I'll be perfectly safe with George, Eileen, and Luke Ventura there.

"Okay," she told Noah after a minute. "It's a date."

Noah beamed. "You won't regret this, Nancy."

Joe felt uneasy as he watched the polo players taking the field for the fourth chukker. His instinct told him that something was off. But what?

It had nothing to do with the polo players or with the match itself. Joe was having an excellent time: his chair was comfortable, the view was perfect, and the waiters kept plying him with hors d'oeuvres. And even though he didn't quite understand polo, he enjoyed the way it looked— elegant and old-fashioned, definitely a game from another time.

No, Joe's bad feeling was totally unrelated to the match. It had to do with the fact that Marco

Donatelli's murder, the poison dart incident, and the attack against Brigitte Bouvier had occurred in very public places. The person responsible was on a roll, and it was more than possible that he or she was getting ready to strike again, right here at the polo grounds.

Joe glanced around. Frank was sitting next to him, talking to Mr. Fairfield. In front of Joe were Prince Zafir and his two bodyguards. Chelsea Vaughn, who looked really cute in a yellow sundress, stood next to her father.

Joe knew that Brigitte was at her hotel, recovering from that afternoon's chloroform encounter. And where was Luke Ventura? Joe wondered. He had been sitting next to Chelsea, but now he wasn't there. Joe and Frank intended to question the young actor about the events of the past two days. They also intended to talk to Prince Zafir as soon as they could get him away from his musclemen.

A pony galloped by, just ten feet in front of where the Fairfield party was sitting. Its rider swung his polo mallet in a graceful arc and sent the ball flying toward the goal. It went in, and the crowd clapped politely.

"Another canapé, sir?" A waiter was bending toward Joe and holding out his tray.

"No, thanks," Joe told him. He turned to Frank, who was watching the polo players regroup in the middle of the field. "Have you seen Luke Ventura?" he whispered.

"He got up a few minutes ago," Frank whispered back. "He's probably stretching his legs." He added, "There's a break in the match coming up. We can talk to him then."

Joe nodded in the direction of Prince Zafir. "And what about the prince? When are we going to talk to him? Those goons of his are glued to—"

But he never finished his sentence. At that very second a shot rang out. Right in front of him, the champagne glass Prince Zafir was holding shattered into a hundred pieces.

Chapter

Twelve

J OE REACTED instantaneously. He dove for the ground. Out of the corner of his eye he saw Frank do the same.

"Get down!" Joe shouted to everyone around him. But pandemonium had erupted. People were screaming and running from their seats. The polo ponies, spooked by the sound of the gunshot, were whinnying frantically.

Joe glanced anxiously at the prince. He was lying utterly still on the ground, next to his two bodyguards.

Joe crept forward, keeping his head down. He managed to make eye contact with one of the bodyguards. "Is the prince okay?" he asked, then realized the guard probably didn't understand him.

"I am perfectly fine, Mr. Hardy," came the prince's voice. "Just a little uncomfortable."

Joe let out a sigh of relief. "Good," he said. "Stay put, then. Don't move."

Frank had Mr. Fairfield's cellular phone in hand and was calling the police. When he'd hung up, Joe said, "I'm going to try to figure out where that shot came from."

"Be careful," Frank told him. "I think I'll stick around here to make sure no one was hurt."

Joe nodded, then got to his feet. He kept his knees bent and his body low. He remembered hearing the shot being fired from somewhere behind the seats, so he headed in that direction.

He paused for a second and assessed the situation. There was a small, grassy area near the seats, and beyond that, a wire fence and the parking lot. The sniper could be hiding behind a parked car, Joe thought, although chances were good that he or she had taken the one shot and beaten it out of there, fast.

Joe hustled over to the parking lot and started walking alongside the fence. Even though the lot was full of cars, there was not a person in sight. Still, Joe glanced to his right and left with every step. He had no interest in being a sitting duck for some trigger-happy maniac.

Finally, he reached the part of the fence directly in line with Prince Zafir's seat. There was no car parked in front of it. Joe noted that it was the only empty spot in an otherwise full parking lot. Interesting, he thought.

He hunched down on his knees and began exploring the ground. He found several old cigarette butts, a red ticket stub from the previous week's polo matches, and a balled-up napkin. Everything was dirty and covered with grime. Yuck, Joe thought. I feel like a garbage collector.

Then something glistening caught his eye. In a tuft of grass next to the fence was a small button. It was silver with a leaf design etched into it.

Joe noticed that there was a tiny sliver of thread attached to the button. The thread was totally white, not dirty at all, which meant that it must have fallen off its owner's clothing very recently.

"Bingo," Joe said out loud, pocketing the button.

Joe headed back to where Frank was standing. A guy with a first-aid kit was there helping some people who'd been cut by the shattered glass. Mr. Fairfield was on the phone, barking orders at somebody.

"Any luck?" Frank asked Joe in a low voice.

Joe showed him the button. "It might be nothing. On the other hand, it might be a clue to our psycho killer."

"Way to go," Frank told him. He looked thoughtful. "Although since the prince was just targeted, I guess he's off our suspect list."

"I guess so," Joe agreed. "And if we go with

our theory that the killer is after all of Goldenrod's potential bidders, then that leaves just one person: Luke Ventura—"

"Who isn't here," Frank finished, glancing around. "He seems to have left the polo grounds." He added, "The other possibility is that Luke isn't our killer at all but the next target. Although it doesn't look too good for him that he disappeared just minutes before the shot was fired."

Nancy set her blanket down on the wide lawn of the Saratoga Performing Arts Center. "Perfect," she said, gazing down the crowded hill at the SPAC pavilion. "The view is great. We'll be able to see the whole orchestra."

It was a beautiful, balmy evening. Hundreds of people were sitting on the lawn, enjoying picnics by candlelight. The twilight sky was a wash with apricot and gold.

"This place is so cool!" George exclaimed.

"Jimmy and I come here all the time," Eileen said. "I don't know much about classical music, but he's an expert." She smiled wistfully, and her eyes filled with tears.

Nancy gave Eileen a hug. "Hang in there," Nancy said. "We'll find Jimmy."

Eileen nodded and wiped away her tears. "I was going to cancel out on you guys, but then I decided it was better to be with you than sitting home alone!"

"I think you definitely made the right choice," George said as the three girls sat down on the blanket.

She looked around. "Luke should be here soon. He's coming straight from the polo match."

"Noah's meeting us, too," Nancy added. "He'd better get here soon—he's bringing dinner." She turned to Eileen. "Actually, it's just as well that we're alone for a bit. I know it's hard for you, but we need to talk about the case."

Eileen toyed with one of her gold studs. "I couldn't believe it when you called me last night and told me about the note, the knife, and the threatening phone call. Why would someone go to all that trouble to keep you from finding Jimmy?"

"I don't know," Nancy replied. "But it makes me think that Jimmy's disappearance isn't connected to the petty cash theft. It seems more likely that Jimmy was kidnapped and that his kidnapper or kidnappers don't want me to track him down."

"Kidnapped," Eileen echoed with a shudder. "I don't like the sound of that."

"Neither do I," Nancy said. "But listen, there's more."

She proceeded to tell Eileen about her conversation with Popeye Lopez. When she'd finished, Eileen looked agitated. "It sounds like this Popeye person is hiding something about Jimmy. We have to find him and make him tell us what it is!"

"That's easier said than done," George spoke up. "We have no idea where he lives."

Eileen gasped suddenly. "Oh, I totally forgot. Where is my brain these days?" She reached into her black leather backpack and pulled out a piece of paper. "I found this in a book Jimmy left at my apartment," she told Nancy. "I wasn't sure if it was important, but I figured I should show it to you."

Nancy took the piece of paper from Eileen. On it was some scratchy writing that she recognized as Jimmy's. It said:

> ADD FM
> KATIE
> PAT
> SON

At the bottom of the piece of paper were the words *SECRET DEAL???* underlined three times in red.

Nancy felt a thrill of excitement. Her instincts told her that this piece of paper was a valuable clue.

"Do you have any idea what this means?" Nancy asked Eileen.

Eileen shrugged. "It's Greek to me."

"Do you suppose it's in code?" George asked, peering over Nancy's shoulder.

"Good evening, ladies."

Nancy glanced up. Noah was standing there. He was dressed in jeans and a black T-shirt, and he was holding a large picnic basket.

He sat down next to Nancy. "I hope you're all hungry," he said cheerfully. He opened the basket and began pulling things out of it. "Plates, napkins, baguettes, cheese, paté," he rattled off. "Pasta salad, grapes, raspberry cheesecake, mineral water, and sodas. And of course, a little atmosphere." He set a candle and a single red rose in a bud vase on top of the picnic basket.

Despite her doubts about Noah, Nancy couldn't help but smile. "That's pretty amazing," she said.

Noah smiled at her. "I'm glad you think so."

A moment later Luke came rushing up to the group. "I'm sorry I'm late," he said breathlessly. He grinned at George. "I hope I didn't keep you waiting too long."

"No problem," George told him. She introduced him to Nancy, Eileen, and Noah.

"We met at my father's party," Noah said, shaking Luke's hand.

Luke sat down next to George. Nancy thought that he looked really handsome in jeans and a long-sleeved white linen shirt with silver buttons.

The five of them began eating. The musicians came on stage and started warming up. The sounds of strings, woodwinds, and brass instruments filled the air, creating a rich tapestry of sound.

While Luke, George, and Eileen were talking about the evening's program, Nancy took the opportunity to show Noah the piece of paper Eileen had found. If the piece of paper was connected to Jimmy's disappearance and Noah was involved, then she might get an interesting reaction out of him.

"Do these words and letters mean anything to you?" Nancy asked him.

Noah bent his head close to hers and peered intently at the paper. Nancy watched him carefully.

"This is definitely Jimmy's handwriting," Noah said after a moment. "But as for what it all means . . ." He shrugged and shook his head.

Nancy stared at him. As far as she could tell, he seemed to be telling the truth. On the other hand, she thought, he could be a good actor.

"Hey, Noah! How's it going, man?"

Nancy looked up and saw a young guy with dreadlocks standing over their blanket.

"Uh, hi, Raphael," Noah said. He looked extremely uncomfortable all of a sudden.

"Hey, Noah, man," Raphael said. "I want a rematch for last night. Maybe later on? Sharkey's Pool Hall?"

"Not tonight," Noah told him nervously. "Listen, I'll talk to you later, okay?"

When Raphael had gone, Nancy turned to look at Noah. "I thought you were sick last night," she said.

"I *was,*" Noah insisted. "Raphael was thinking about the night before. He had it all mixed up. Here, do you want another piece of Jarlsberg?"

Without waiting for her reply, Noah began slicing some cheese. Nancy watched him suspiciously. It was obvious he was lying. But why?

The audience began clapping, startling Nancy out of her thoughts. The conductor was walking onto the stage.

A moment later, the concert began. Nancy tried to enjoy the music—a Beethoven symphony—but it was hard. Her mind was in a turmoil about Noah. On the one hand, she didn't have any real proof that he'd kidnapped Jimmy. On the other hand, the fact that he seemed to be lying about his whereabouts the night before was not a good sign. Plus, there was the business of the Billie Holiday song. . . . But what could be his motive? she wondered.

She glanced at George, who was sitting next to Luke. The two of them were whispering about something and laughing. Nancy was happy for George; she and Luke seemed to be having a great time together. Eileen, who was sitting in front of Nancy, was staring moodily off into space. She must be thinking about Jimmy, Nancy thought sympathetically.

After the concert was over, the five of them

packed up Noah's picnic basket and headed to the parking lot. Everyone else was leaving at the same time, and the main path was wall-to-wall with people.

Because of the massive crowd, Nancy and Eileen found themselves separated from George, Noah, and Luke. Nancy could see them up ahead, in front of a large group of senior citizens. "Meet you out in the parking lot!" Nancy called out to her friends.

George glanced over her shoulder and waved. "Okay!"

The path turned into a bridge. Nancy inched over to the metal railing and peered over. About a hundred feet below was a ravine with some interesting-looking mineral formations. Nancy knew that the park in which the arts center was housed was full of natural mineral springs. Other people were standing at the railing, jostling one another, trying to get a view.

Then Nancy turned to Eileen, who was standing right behind her. "Let me ask you a question," she said in a low voice. "How well do you know Noah?"

Eileen grinned. "Why? Are you interested in him?"

"No," Nancy replied quickly. "I'm wondering if there's a chance he might have been involved in Jimmy's disappearance."

Eileen jaw dropped, then she began laughing. "Oh, no way. They're really good friends."

"Are you sure?" Nancy pressed.

"Absolutely," Eileen replied. "Noah may have his problems, but being a kidnapper is definitely not one of them." Her gaze wandered. "Hey, I see someone from Lulu's. I'm going to try to catch up with him and say hi, okay? I'll meet you out in the parking lot."

"Okay," Nancy said.

Eileen squeezed through the crowd and disappeared. Nancy cast one last glance over the railing at the rock formations, then decided to start back to the parking lot. But it was almost impossible to move. People were bumping into her from all sides; it was like being on a subway platform at rush hour.

Just then she felt a pair of hands grab her from behind. Before she could react, she was lifted off her feet. Someone was trying to shove her over the edge of the railing into the ravine below!

Chapter

Thirteen

NANCY SCREAMED as she felt herself being pushed over the railing. At the same instant, whoever was pushing her suddenly let go. Nancy grabbed the railing, forced her body back, and regained her balance. Then she whirled around to see who had attacked her.

But all she saw were the concerned faces of several old ladies. "Are you all right, dear?" one of them murmured.

"Did you see who pushed me?" Nancy asked them quickly.

The old ladies looked at one another, puzzled. "No," one of them said after a moment. The others shook their heads.

Confused, Nancy glanced around. Masses of

people continued to walk across the bridge, staring curiously at her. Was one of them her attacker? She didn't recognize any of their faces.

Then she saw Eileen squeezing past some people toward her. "Are you okay?" she demanded. "I heard you scream."

"I'm fine," Nancy reassured her. "Someone tried to push me over the railing."

"What!" Eileen gasped.

Seconds later George, Noah, and Luke managed to reach Nancy as well. She repeated her story to them.

Nancy's friends fussed over her for a while, but she convinced them that she was okay. As the group started toward the parking lot again, Nancy leaned toward George. "You heard me scream, right?" she whispered.

George nodded. "I couldn't miss it."

"Was Noah with you at the time?" Nancy asked her.

"Yeah," George replied without hesitation. "He and Luke and I have been together since we left the lawn. We were talking about Luke's new movie." She added, "Who do you think tried to push you, Nan?"

"I don't know," Nancy said slowly.

As she walked, Nancy wondered if her assailant was the same guy who had broken into their hotel room. "Stop looking for Jimmy or you'll end up like Marco," his note had said. "I'd hate to have to kill a pretty girl like you," he'd warned her on the phone. If he was the one, he sure wasn't wasting any time. And he definitely hadn't been making idle threats.

In any case, Nancy mused, Noah couldn't have been the one who tried to push her over the railing. Did that mean he wasn't guilty of any of the other stuff? Nancy asked herself.

The next morning the Hardys, Nancy, and George met at Lulu's Coffeehouse for breakfast. Lulu's was a small, cozy café with mismatched tables and murals with nineteenth-century horse-racing scenes. Eileen was behind the counter, working the espresso machine. A reggae song was playing on the radio.

Nancy took a sip of her cappuccino, then turned to Frank and Joe. She was glad to be able to spend some time with the brothers, whom she hadn't seen since Oliver Fairfield's party. "So tell us what's going on with your case," she said. "The yearling auction is this afternoon, right?"

Frank took a swallow of his orange juice, then said, "Right. But there's a lot of other stuff going on, too. Yesterday morning Mr. Fairfield hired us to investigate Marco Donatelli's murder. Then Goldenrod got plugged by a cyanide-laced dart, although he recovered, thanks to Eileen's brother Sean. We think the assailant was aiming at Wyatt Vaughn, who's one of Goldenrod's potential bidders."

"There's more," Joe continued. "Brigitte

Bouvier was grabbed from behind and chloroformed while she was walking around the racetrack yesterday afternoon. And last evening someone took a shot at Prince Zafir at the polo match. At least we *think* the person was aiming at the prince. Anyway, the prince wasn't hurt, and neither was anyone else."

"The police found the bullet," Frank added. "It came from a nine-millimeter Luger."

"That happened yesterday evening?" Nancy said, surprised. She turned to George. "I wonder why Luke didn't mention it. He came to the arts center from the polo match, right?"

Joe practically choked on his double espresso. "You saw Luke Ventura last night?" he sputtered. "Where? What time? What kind of car was he driving?"

George frowned. "Hey, why are you acting all weird about Luke? Maybe he left the match before the shooting."

"Was Luke wearing a shirt or a jacket with silver buttons?" Frank asked the girls.

Nancy wondered where the Hardys' line of questioning was leading. "Actually, he was," she replied. "A long-sleeved white linen shirt. Why?"

Frank and Joe looked at each other. "Oh boy," Frank muttered. "Joe found a silver button at a spot where the sniper could have been standing. It was small, with a leaf design etched into it."

"I don't know if Luke's buttons had leaves etched on them," Nancy admitted. "I didn't look that closely." She added, "Luke is really a suspect?"

"Oh, no way," George said incredulously. "He's a famous movie star, plus one of the nicest people I've ever met. You honestly think he could be a murderer?"

"We just want to talk to the guy, that's all," Joe reassured her. "It's possible that our hit man— excuse me, hit person—is going after all of Goldenrod's potential bidders: Marco, Mr. Vaughn, Brigitte, and now Prince Zafir. Luke's the only one left."

"Are you thinking he's trying to get rid of the competition?" Nancy asked the Hardys.

"It's a possibility," Frank replied. "It's also possible that he's the next victim."

Nancy took a bite of her lemon-poppyseed muffin. "You said you weren't sure Prince Zafir was the target yesterday evening, right?" she said after a moment. "Who was sitting near him?"

"His hired muscle was on either side of him," Joe replied. "And we were behind him."

"So maybe the assailant was going after the two of you," George pointed out. "You know, to keep you from finding out who killed Marco and who shot the cyanide-laced dart at Goldenrod or Mr. Vaughn and also to keep you from discovering who chloroformed Brigitte Bouvier."

"That's true," Frank conceded.

Joe grinned at Nancy and George. "So enough about us. What's going on with your case?"

Nancy told the brothers about the hotel break-in, the threatening call, and the incident at the arts center. She also mentioned her run-in with Popeye Lopez at the track and her suspicions about Noah.

"Although I'm not so sure about Noah now," Nancy finished. "There's no way he could have tried to push me over the railing. It had to have been someone else."

Just then, the door to the coffeehouse opened, and a balding, middle-aged man walked in. He went up to the counter and ordered some muffins to go from Eileen.

"That guy looks familiar," Nancy said to her friends. "Who is he?"

"That's Abe Addison of Addison Farms," Joe told her. "He's the one who's selling Goldenrod at the yearling auction this afternoon."

"Addison Farms," Nancy repeated slowly. The words triggered something in her brain.

Then it came to her. "Addison Farms—that's it!" she exclaimed.

"What's it?" Frank asked her.

Nancy reached into her shoulder bag and pulled out the piece of paper Eileen had found in Jimmy's book. She explained where it had come from to the Hardys, then pointed to the first five letters. "*ADD FM* might stand for Addison Farms," she said excitedly.

Frank pointed to the words *Katie, Pat, and son.* "And what about this other stuff?" he asked.

"Maybe Katie and Pat are relatives or friends of Abe Addison's—or maybe they're his employees," George suggested. "As for son—maybe that's somebody's son."

"And the three of them are in on a secret deal?" Joe said skeptically. "I don't know. That's a lot to assume from the letters *ADD FM*. For all you know, they don't even stand for Addison Farms."

Nancy glanced up to see if Mr. Addison was still there. He wasn't. She rose from her seat, went to the door, and looked outside. The horse breeder was nowhere in sight.

Nancy returned to her table. "I think this is worth checking out," she told her friends. "Maybe you and I should head out to Addison Farms this morning, George."

"And we have to go find Luke," Joe said to Frank. He turned to George. "You seem pretty tight with the dude, George. Do you have any idea where he is this morning?"

"He's hanging out at the Victoria Pool, if you must know," George replied hesitantly. "I'm supposed to meet him there later on. But you guys are wasting your time. He's innocent!"

"We'll see," Joe said.

"I just thought of something," Nancy said. She held up the piece of paper and looked pointedly at the Hardys. "There's a chance Addison Farms is a clue to Jimmy's disappearance, right? And your theories about Marco Donatelli's murder and the other stuff have to do with Goldenrod, who's owned by Abe Addison." She added, "Do you suppose our two cases might be connected?"

Frank and Joe exchanged glances. "Definitely," they said at the same time.

Addison Farms was on the outskirts of Saratoga, about two miles away from the Fairfield estate. The property consisted of a large, slightly run-down Victorian house, a number of red barns, and many acres of green meadows with horses grazing on them.

"I wonder if Mr. Addison will be here," George remarked as she and Nancy drove up the driveway. "We did just see him in town, after all."

"Well, even if he's not here, someone else might be able to help us," Nancy pointed out.

Nancy parked in front of the house and stepped out of the car. She went up to a young guy who was trimming the hedges. "Hi," she called out. "Is Mr. Addison around?"

"I think he's out back some place," the guy replied without glancing up.

Nancy and George headed to the far stables. After searching around for a moment, they found Mr. Addison near one of the barns, tending to a delicate-looking brown filly. He was crouched down on the ground, inspecting her shins.

When he saw the girls, he stood up and wiped

his brow with the back of his hand. "Looking for someone?" he asked them.

"We're looking for you, actually," Nancy said. She introduced herself and George. "We saw you at Lulu's Coffeehouse a little while ago."

"Oh, right," Mr. Addison said, nodding. "I noticed you two. You were sitting with those boys who work for Mr. Fairfield." He added, "I was at the Fairfield paddocks this morning, checking on my yearlings. The auction's this afternoon, and there're a million things to do." He sounded friendly, but his tone implied that he was way too busy to chat with Nancy and George.

"We'll get right to the point," Nancy said crisply. "We're looking for Jimmy English, who's been missing since Wednesday."

"Jimmy English, Jimmy English." Mr. Addison scratched his chin. "Don't recall the name. Oh, no, that's not true. He's the fellow who reviews movies for the *Sentinel,* right?"

"Actually, he's one of their reporters," George spoke up. "Anyway, we came across a clue that might help us track him down. It has to do with this farm, and some people named Katie and Pat."

"Do you know anybody with those names?" Nancy added. "Like friends, relatives, or employees?"

Mr. Addison suddenly looked uncomfortable. Nancy wondered what had triggered it.

"Um, no," he said after a moment. His eyes were averted, and he sounded nervous. "What is this clue you're talking about? Something that involves my farm?"

Nancy showed him the piece of paper with Jimmy's scribblings on it. Mr. Addison's hand shook as he took it from her. He stared at it blankly, then handed it back to Nancy. "I don't understand. Is this supposed to mean something to me?"

"This was found in Jimmy's things," Nancy explained, "and we were wondering if it might be connected to his disappearance somehow."

"I'm afraid I can't help you," Mr. Addison told her. "There's no one here by the name of Katie or Pat." He reached into his pocket, pulled out a bottle of pills, and popped one into his mouth. "I've got a bad ulcer," he explained.

Just then a young woman came rushing up to Mr. Addison. "Phone call for you, Dad," she told him. "I think it's Sean."

"Thanks, Annie," Mr. Addison said. "Sorry I couldn't be of more help," he told Nancy and George. Then he turned and hurried into the house.

Nancy watched him go. Her instincts told her that he'd been lying. What was he hiding?

"Excuse me," she called out to Mr. Addison's daughter, who was about to follow her father into the house.

Annie Addison smiled at her. "Yes?"

"It's too complicated to go into, but we're looking for some people named Katie and Pat who might work here," Nancy explained. "Or maybe they're friends or relatives of your dad's—I don't know."

Annie broke into a laugh. "You're looking for Katie and Pat?"

Nancy's heart skipped a beat. Annie was going to tell her who they were! "Yes. Can you help us?"

"Sure," Annie replied merrily. "But you should know—you're looking for a couple of horses, not people."

"Horses?" George repeated, confused.

"That's right," Annie said. "Katie My Love and Pat on the Back. They're stabled in Barn Five."

The Victoria Pool was an elegant outdoor pool nestled in the heart of Spa Park. By the time Frank and Joe got there, there were dozens of people sunbathing on the teakwood chaise longues, and a few swimming in the water.

Joe glanced around, enjoying the scenery. There sure are a lot of beautiful women in Saratoga, he thought. "I wish I'd brought my trunks," he told Frank wistfully.

"We're not here to do laps, bro. We're here to talk to Luke," Frank reminded him. "Speaking of which—there he is on the diving board. Come on."

Frank and Joe walked over to the deep end. Luke was poised on the diving board, his eyes closed, his face a mask of concentration. Then he opened his eyes, pushed off with his feet, and executed a perfect jackknife into the water.

Seconds later the young actor rose to the surface and swam leisurely to the edge. Frank and Joe were waiting for him.

"Hi, how's it going?" Frank called out, smiling.

"Oh, hi," Luke said breathlessly. He grabbed the edge of the pool and hoisted himself up. Drops of water ran down his face and body. "Frank and Joe, right?"

"Right," Joe said cheerfully. "You're a pretty awesome diver."

"Thanks," Luke said, looking pleased. "I was on the diving team in high school. It's about the only sport I'm really good at."

Joe was struck by how modest and normal Luke sounded. After all, he *was* a megastar.

Okay, enough of the admiration society, Joe thought. Time to get the ball rolling. "It's a bummer what happened at the polo match yesterday evening, isn't it?" he said.

Luke wandered over to a nearby chair, picked up a white towel, and wrapped it around his tanned shoulders. "Yeah," he replied. "I heard about it this morning from Mr. Vaughn."

"You mean you weren't there when the shot

was fired?" Frank said innocently. "I thought I saw you around."

Luke shook his head. "I had to get over to SPAC to meet some friends. I left the polo match after the third chucky. . . . Is that the right word?"

"Chukker," Joe corrected him. He decided to take a different tack. "So, are you psyched about the auction this afternoon?"

Luke's eyes lit up. "Are you kidding? It's all I've been thinking about this morning. I can't tell you guys how much I want to be the high bidder on Goldenrod." He added, "I've loved horse-racing ever since I was a kid. And Goldenrod is a really special horse."

"A lot of people seem to think so," Frank observed.

Just then Joe noticed a familiar figure on the other side of the pool, sunbathing on one of the chaise longues. Long auburn hair, hot pink bikini, black shades . . .

Unless he was mistaken, it was Chelsea.

"By the way, we found a silver button under your chair yesterday evening," Frank was saying to Luke. "Is it yours?"

Luke frowned. "Let's see, what was I wearing yesterday? My white linen shirt." He smiled and shrugged. "I guess I could be missing a button. I'll check when I get back to my hotel room."

"Excuse me," Joe said to Frank and Luke. "I'll

be right back. There's someone I need to say hi to."

Frank shot him a dirty look, but Joe ignored it and hurried to the other side of the pool.

Chelsea was deeply engrossed in a paperback novel called *Passion's Promise* and didn't notice Joe approaching. In one swift motion, he ripped the book out of her hands.

"Hey!" Chelsea protested.

Joe began reading aloud in a very serious tone of voice. " 'Lord Pennington took Belinda in his arms and kissed her on the lips. She couldn't resist him—and yet she knew she had to. She pulled back with a look of fury in her violet eyes and slapped him, hard. "How dare you!" she cried out. "You know I've been promised to Major Jarvis!" ' "

Chelsea frowned. "Joe Hardy! You give that back to me right this second!"

Grinning, Joe handed the book back to her. Chelsea stuffed it into a white canvas bag that was on the ground beside her chair.

She took off her sunglasses and pouted at Joe. "What are you doing, sneaking up on me?" she asked.

"I wasn't sneaking up on you. I just came to say hi." He nodded at the empty chaise next to hers. "Mind if I join you?"

"Actually, that seat's taken," Chelsea told him apologetically.

Unexpectedly, Joe felt a twinge of jealousy. "Oh?"

"That is my chair," came a voice from behind him. "Chelsea was kind enough to save it for me."

Joe turned around. Brigitte Bouvier was standing there. She was wearing a white bikini with a white mesh coverup over it, and she was carrying a white canvas bag. Her hair was swept up under a large straw hat.

"You two are here together?" Joe asked.

"We're staying at the same hotel," Brigitte explained. "I heard Chelsea say to her father that she wanted to come here this morning. I was coming here as well, and so of course I offered her a ride."

Joe nodded. "So how are you feeling? Are you totally recovered from yesterday afternoon?"

Brigitte sat down in her chaise and set her bag down on the ground. "You are very sweet to ask," she said, crossing her slim legs. "I feel much better. I got much sleep, drank much mineral water, and took much aspirins." She added, "Of course, I am glad I missed the polo match. I heard about what happened to the poor prince of Morocco."

"Have you seen the prince around this morning?" Joe asked her.

"I heard that his bodyguards are keeping him out of sight until the auction," Brigitte replied.

"And immediately after the auction, he plans to fly back to Marrakech on his private jet."

"I'm going to get a soda," Chelsea said suddenly, standing up. "Anyone want anything?"

"I'll come with you," Joe told her.

"I do not need anything, thank you," Brigitte said, lying back in her chaise and closing her eyes. "Just a little nap, perhaps. Ah, this sun feels *très bon.*"

Chelsea grabbed her bag from the ground and started walking toward the concession stand. Joe followed her. He was trying very hard not to stare at her too much. She looked incredibly cute in her hot pink bikini.

"So," Joe managed to say after a moment, "are you excited about the auction?"

"Oh, I'm so *nervous,*" Chelsea told him. "I want Goldenrod so badly. I just know Daddy's going to get outbid, though."

"What makes you so sure?" Joe asked her.

"I'm *not* sure," Chelsea admitted. "But I don't want to get my hopes up."

When they got to the concession stand, Chelsea pulled her wallet out of her bag. "Let's see. Do I want a root beer float or a strawberry milkshake? Definitely some fries. We could split them or something. . . ." Then she frowned at her wallet. "Hey, this isn't mine!"

"Huh?" Joe asked her.

Chelsea opened up the wallet. "Here's some stuff in French— Oh, I get it. This must be Ms.

Bouvier's." She held up the white canvas bag. "Our bags are almost exactly the same. I must have picked hers up by mistake."

But Joe wasn't listening to her. He was staring at a familiar-looking red stub sticking out of Brigitte's wallet.

"Here, give me that," Joe said, taking the wallet from Chelsea. He pulled the red stub out. It was a torn ticket from the previous evening's polo match.

"What is it?" Chelsea asked him. "Joe? Hey, Joe?"

Joe didn't reply. His mind was racing.

Brigitte must have been at the polo match, he thought. No one had seen her there, however, and she'd claimed to have spent the evening resting in her hotel room.

Why had she lied? Joe wondered.

Chapter
Fourteen

THE LIBRARIAN handed Nancy a folder of newspaper clippings. "You can start with these," he told her. "It's everything we have on Addison Farms. Unfortunately, the clippings aren't in any sort of order."

"Thank you," Nancy said. Then she sat down in a nearby chair and began going through them.

After leaving Addison Farms, Nancy had dropped off George at the Victoria Pool to meet Luke. Then she'd decided to do some research at the public library on Addison Farms, Katie My Love, and Pat on the Back. As far as she could tell, something was very fishy. Mr. Addison had withheld information about his two horses from Nancy and George. But why? Nancy had started to ask his daughter Annie more questions about Katie and Pat, but Mr. Addison had poked his head out the door and told her to come into the house.

After half an hour of leafing through clippings, Nancy came across an interesting one. According to this particular article, Katie My Love and Pat on the Back had produced a male foal the previous year who'd died at birth. The attending vet had been somebody named Dr. O'Neill.

Nancy finished going through the rest of the clippings and found nothing else referring to Katie or Pat. She returned to the one about the death of their foal.

Nancy frowned as she reread it. Why had Mr. Addison wanted to hide these facts from her? she wondered. Also, what could the word *son* mean, which Jimmy had scribbled under the others? Had he been referring to Katie and Pat's deceased offspring? But the correct term was *foal*, not *son*.

And how did the whole thing relate to a secret deal? Nancy mused.

Just then the door to the library's periodical room opened, and Tracy Kim walked in. When she saw Nancy, she stopped in her tracks. Nancy realized that she and Tracy were the only people in the room; the librarian was nowhere in sight.

"Hi," Nancy called out. "Fancy meeting you here."

"I—I was delivering some back issues of the *Sentinel* to the librarian," Tracy mumbled, holding up a large manila envelope. She glanced around. "I guess he's not here, so I'll just come back later."

Nancy noticed that Tracy seemed very uncomfortable. She also noticed that the young intern was wearing a really expensive dress. Nancy knew how much it cost because she'd noticed it at one of the downtown boutiques when she was shopping on Thursday afternoon.

How could an unpaid intern at a newspaper afford such pricey clothes? Nancy wondered. Then something clicked in her mind, something she should have seen long ago.

"I just figured it out," Nancy said out loud. *"You* stole the petty cash from the *Sentinel* office, Tracy. And you tried to pin it on Jimmy."

Tracy suddenly looked like a trapped animal. "What are you talking about?" she asked in a trembling voice.

"You made up the story about Jimmy's gambling problem to throw everyone off," Nancy went on. "And you freaked out when I told you I was going to talk to Popeye Lopez. You knew he would expose your lies."

"I *did* see Jimmy talking to Popeye Lopez," Tracy insisted. Then her eyes filled with tears, and she began to cry. "B-but you're right about the rest of it."

Nancy tried to hide her excitement. Tracy was going to confess!

She reached into her purse, pulled out a tissue, and offered it to Tracy. Tracy took it, then sat down in the chair opposite Nancy's and put her head in her hands.

"Why did you do it, Tracy?" Nancy asked her quietly.

"I—I wanted the money," Tracy sputtered between sobs. "I got the intern job because I wanted to break into journalism. But I wasn't prepared for how totally broke I'd be. All my friends are working at the mall and stuff, and they have loads of cash to spend. How was I supposed to keep up with them?"

The librarian returned just then and resumed his position behind his desk. He peered at Nancy and Tracy over the rim of his glasses, then began shuffling some papers.

Nancy lowered her voice and asked, "What made you decide to pin the theft on Jimmy?"

"I took the money on Wednesday night," Tracy explained. "And on Thursday morning, it turned out that Jimmy was missing. The timing seemed perfect. So I made up this story about him having a gambling problem and let everyone else put two and two together."

Nancy nodded. "The stuff about Popeye Lopez—how much of that was true?"

"As I said before, I did see Jimmy talking to him," Tracy replied. "I was kind of curious. I thought, what's Jimmy doing with a sleazebag like Popeye? That's why I told you and everybody else about it. I thought it would make Jimmy look bad. But I didn't think you'd actually chase Popeye down!"

Nancy stared at Tracy, who seemed genuinely distraught and remorseful. She felt sorry for the girl. On the other hand, Tracy had committed a crime—*plus* she'd smeared Jimmy's personal and professional image—and she was going to have to pay for it. "You know, you're going to have to tell your boss and the police all this stuff, don't you?" Nancy told her.

"I know," Tracy said sadly. "I'm sure that'll be the end of my so-called journalism career."

Then Nancy remembered something else. She and George had seen Tracy in the lobby of their hotel on Thursday night just before they'd discovered the knife and the note warning Nancy to stop looking for Jimmy.

"You broke into our hotel room on Thursday night, didn't you?" Nancy demanded. "You claimed you were meeting some friends to hear the jazz quartet, but—"

"No way!" Tracy interrupted. "I absolutely did not break into your hotel room. Why would I do a crazy thing like that?" She dabbed at her eyes with the tissue. "I really *was* meeting some friends, and they really *did* blow me off. If I acted weird when I ran into you and George, it's because I was afraid of the two of you. I thought you were onto me."

Nancy gazed skeptically at Tracy, but the young intern seemed to be sincere. "Okay," Nancy said with a sigh. "One last question: Do you have any idea where Jimmy is now?"

Tracy shook her head. "I'm totally clueless on that one. If he was planning to run away, he didn't let anyone at the paper in on it."

Nancy drove her rental car into the parking lot of the Diamond Spa. She was late for a one o'clock appointment for a mineral bath. Eileen had suggested that they meet there to talk about the case. Nancy hoped she hadn't kept her waiting too long.

Nancy parked the car, grabbed her bathing suit, and went into the beautiful white Victorian building in which the spa was housed. She knew from her guidebooks that Saratoga was known for its natural mineral springs. People had been coming to the town for over a hundred years to seek out the waters' healing properties. Nancy didn't need any healing, but she was definitely psyched for an hour of relaxation.

Inside the building a matronly attendant directed Nancy to a private dressing room. She handed Nancy a white cotton robe and a glass of water. "Drink up," the attendant said. "It's arsenic water."

Nancy started. "What? You mean arsenic, as in *poison?"*

The attendant smiled. "Most of our customers are surprised to hear there's arsenic in the water. But it's a very, very low level, and it won't hurt you at all." She added, "You'll be bathing in water with natural arsenic in it. It's our philosophy here at Diamond Spa that you should drink the water you bathe in for extra curative effect."

Nancy stared doubtfully at the glass. "You're *sure* this won't hurt me?"

"Absolutely," the attendant replied. "Everyone who comes here drinks it. It tastes a little funny, but you'll get used to it."

The attendant left, and Nancy changed into her bathing suit. Then she took a sip of the water. "Yuck," she said out loud. "It doesn't taste funny. It tastes *awful."*

She took a deep breath and finished off the rest of the glass. Then she put on her robe over her suit and proceeded to the bathing area.

Eileen was already there, sitting alone in a large, sunken tub. Her eyes were closed, and her cheeks were flushed pink. Sunlight poured through a skylight, illuminating the tiny, jewel-colored tiles on the floor and walls. The air was steamy and warm and smelled vaguely medicinal.

Eileen opened her eyes and smiled groggily at Nancy. "Hey, come on in. I feel like Jell-O."

"Sorry I'm late," Nancy said. She took her robe off, hung it up on a hook, then slipped into the super-hot water.

As she sat down next to Eileen, she let her shoulders sink down below water level. Tiny bubbles effervesced against her skin; it was like bathing in champagne. "This is pretty great," Nancy said appreciatively.

"Isn't it, though?" Eileen sighed. "I really needed this after everything that's been going on these last few days. When you called me from the library and asked if we could meet, I thought of this place right away." She glanced anxiously at Nancy. "So what do you have to tell me? Do you have some news about Jimmy?"

"Yup," Nancy said, nodding. "And for once, it's good news—well, sort of." Then she proceeded to tell Eileen about her conversation with Tracy.

When she'd finished, Eileen's hazel eyes were blazing with anger. "I can't believe she'd steal the money and try to pin it on Jimmy!" she cried out. "Of all the low-life, lousy things to do!"

"Tracy is going to confess everything to her boss and to the police," Nancy reassured her. "Jimmy's name will be totally cleared."

"It'd better be," Eileen fumed. "Wait till I get my hands on Tracy! I'll wring her neck!"

"That might be hard to do if she goes to jail," Nancy told her. "Listen, there's more. Remember that piece of paper you found in Jimmy's book? I figured out what some of the words on it mean. *ADD FM* is Addison Farms, and *Katie* and *Pat* are two horses Mr. Addison owns named Katie My Love and Pat on the Back."

Eileen frowned. "So Jimmy was working on a story about Addison Farms?"

"I'm not sure," Nancy replied. "I did some research at the library and found out that Katie My Love and Pat on the Back had a foal last year. Some vet named Dr. O'Neill delivered him. Unfortunately, the foal died—"

"What do you mean, some vet named Dr. O'Neill?" Eileen interrupted. She looked amused. "That's my brother Sean you're talking about!"

Nancy was totally confused. "What? I don't understand. Your last name is Reed."

"I guess I didn't explain when I introduced you guys," Eileen said apologetically. "Sean is my half-brother. We have the same mother but different fathers."

"Sean O'Neill," Nancy said under her breath. Then it came to her. The word *son* on the piece of paper was not a word at all, but the initials S-O-N: Sean O'Neill.

Now Nancy was more puzzled than ever. What did Sean have to do with the mystery—if there was one—surrounding Katie My Love and Pat on the Back?

"I'm curious," Nancy said. "What's Sean's connection to Addison Farms?"

"Sean is Mr. Addison's regular vet," Eileen explained. "He takes care of all his horses and delivers all the new foals. In fact, do you know about that famous yearling, Goldenrod—the one that's up for sale this afternoon? Sean delivered him himself in the middle of a horrible thunderstorm."

When Nancy left the spa an hour later, she was still mulling over the Abe Addison–Sean O'Neill connection. She hadn't shared her insight about the letters *SON* with Eileen. For one thing, she didn't want to alarm her friend unnecessarily. For another thing, she wasn't sure there was anything to get alarmed about.

Nancy opened the door to her car and climbed in. There was a bottle of mineral water that she'd bought at lunchtime laying on the passenger seat. She grabbed it and took a long swig. The bath had been relaxing, but she felt hot and flushed. And of course, the August heat didn't help.

Almost immediately Nancy stopped drinking and frowned at the bottle. The water tasted funny, sort of like the arsenic water she'd drunk before her bath. "I must be imagining things," she said to herself. "It tasted fine earlier."

Shrugging, Nancy set the bottle down and

started the car. It was time to figure out her next move. She had to find Sean and talk to him. Even if he wasn't connected to Jimmy's disappearance, he might be able to answer some questions, she realized.

But Sean—and Mr. Addison—weren't the only suspicious figures in her case, Nancy reminded herself. There were also unresolved issues involving Popeye Lopez and Noah. Even though Tracy had absolved Popeye of being Jimmy's bookie, there was no denying his strange behavior on Friday afternoon at the racetrack. When Nancy had told him about Jimmy's disappearance, Popeye had seemed very afraid. What was he hiding?

And what about Noah? she wondered. If nothing else, he'd lied to her about why he'd left his father's party early. What was going on with him?

Still, Nancy wanted to focus on finding Sean right now. She would start with his home and office, then perhaps Addison Farms again and the Fairfield paddocks.

Nancy drove to the end of the spa's parking lot, which emptied into a busy street. But all of a sudden she was seized by an excruciating pain in her stomach. *"Ow!"* she cried out, slamming on the brake. "What was *that?*"

The pain disappeared, but not for long. It came back again seconds later, worse than before. Nancy was also hit with a wave of dizziness and nausea. Beads of sweat broke out on her forehead, and she felt as though she was going to pass out. She groaned and doubled over onto the steering wheel, totally losing sight of where she was or what she was doing.

Without her knowing it, her foot slipped off the brake, and the car rolled forward into the busy street.

Chapter
Fifteen

NANCY HEARD the sound of blaring horns coming from all directions. She clutched her stomach and sat up in her seat. Where was she? she wondered groggily. Then she realized that she was behind the wheel of her car, which was nosing slowly into a heavily congested street.

"Oh, no!" Nancy cried out, stepping on the brake. The car lurched violently and came to a halt just inches away from a red convertible.

The driver of the convertible leaned out of his seat. "Look where you're going!" he shouted. "What's wrong with you, anyway?"

"I—need—a—doctor!" Nancy managed to shout before another terrible wave of pain hit her, and then she passed out.

* * *

When Nancy came to, she found herself lying on a cot, staring up at a strange man with kindly blue eyes. "W-where am I?" she murmured. "And why does my stomach hurt so much?"

"You're in an outpatient clinic," the man told her. "I'm Dr. Lima. A fellow named Henderson brought you in about half an hour ago and said to tell you he parked your car in the spa parking lot."

Nancy glanced around the room, at the beige walls and fluorescent lights and steel sink. "What's wrong with me?" she asked.

The doctor put his fingers on her wrist and glanced at his watch. "You tell me. You say your stomach hurts?"

"Yes," Nancy said. "Plus, I'm dizzy, and my skin feels clammy. It all happened when I was driving out of the parking lot at the Diamond Spa."

"I see," Dr. Lima said, nodding. "What have you had to eat and drink today?"

Nancy frowned, trying to remember. "I had breakfast at Lulu's Coffeehouse—a lemon-poppyseed muffin and a cappuccino. For lunch I grabbed a tuna salad sandwich at some deli. And just now, at the Diamond Spa, I had a glass of arsenic water and then a few sips of some bottled water that I'd bought at the deli."

"Ah, yes, the famous arsenic water," the doctor said with a smile. "There's no way you took in enough arsenic from that to make you ill like this. Although interestingly enough, the symptoms you describe could be attributed to arsenic poisoning."

As Nancy listened to him, she flashed back to the moment when she had climbed into her car and taken a swig of the bottled water. It had tasted strange—like arsenic, she'd thought at the time.

Then an awful thought occurred to her. What if someone had slipped arsenic into her bottled water?

"Dr. Lima, can you test me for arsenic poisoning?" Nancy asked him quickly. "It's a long story, and I'll tell you about it later. But for now I just want to rule it out."

"Certainly," Dr. Lima told her, looking puzzled. "I'll draw some blood right away. And in the meantime, I'll give you something to relieve your pain."

A short while later, Dr. Lima got the test results back from the lab. Nancy's hunch was correct: there was a very low level of arsenic in her blood.

"This is most peculiar," Dr. Lima told her, frowning at the piece of paper in his hands. "I've had the water at the spa myself. There's absolutely no way it could have put this much arsenic into your system."

"I don't think it was the water at the spa," Nancy told him gravely. "I think someone decided to slip some arsenic into the bottled water I had in my car."

"What?" the doctor exclaimed. He shook his head. "I'd like to ask you more questions, but this isn't the time. Right now I need to start your treatment. Fortunately, you ingested only a tiny amount of the poison. A large dose could have been fatal."

An hour later Nancy felt much better. Dr. Lima had given her some medicine to counteract the effects of the arsenic. "I'm going to release you if you promise to take a cab back to your hotel and get plenty of rest," he told her sternly. "Your body's had quite a shock, and it needs to recover. You also need to report this incident to the police."

"No problem," Nancy said. Testing her strength, she rose slowly from the cot. Aside from a little dizziness and some mild cramping, she was definitely on the mend. "Is it okay if I use your phone?"

Dr. Lima scribbled something on the paper on his clipboard, then nodded at a phone on the wall. "Be my guest. I'll be back in a minute to check you out."

When he'd left, Nancy called for a cab. Then she hung up and dialed Eileen's number. Eileen picked up on the first ring. "Hello?"

"Hi, Eileen, this is Nancy," she said in a low voice. "Listen, did you happen to mention to anyone that we were meeting at the spa?"

"Uh, no," Eileen said, sounding confused. "Why do you ask?"

But before Nancy could explain, Eileen cut her off. "Oh, no, there *was* someone. Sean was here with me when you called from the library. I told him where we were going."

Sean again, Nancy thought grimly. She'd bought the bottle of water between leaving the library and arriving at the spa. It was possible that Sean had driven to the spa, seen the bottle in her car, and thought of slipping some arsenic into it. She had been in the spa building for over an hour. There would have been plenty of time to get the arsenic, break into her car, and put the poison into the bottle—a macabre takeoff on the spa's therapy. But why? Nancy wondered.

Eileen's voice cut into her thoughts. "Nancy? Why are you asking me this? What's going on?"

"I'll explain later," Nancy told her. "Right now there's someone I need to talk to."

Joe tapped his foot restlessly. He and Frank were in a nook outside Brigitte's hotel room, hiding behind a potted palm tree. They'd been there for what seemed like forever.

"Hey, bro?" Frank whispered. "Could you stop fidgeting so much? You're making me nervous."

"Whose dumb idea was it to break into her room, anyway?" Joe mumbled.

Frank threw him an exasperated look. "Yours.

You found the stub from the polo match in her wallet. *You* decided that Brigitte could be systematically eliminating the competition for Goldenrod, including Marco, Mr. Vaughn, Prince Zafir—and maybe Luke Ventura next. You also decided that she could have faked the attack on herself at the racetrack. And because of all this, you somehow convinced me to hang out here waiting for Brigitte to leave so we could search her room for incriminating evidence."

"I can see that you're not totally thrilled with this plan," Joe observed. "Listen, if she'd only stayed at the Victoria Pool with Chelsea, this would have been a piece of cake."

"Maybe." Frank glanced at his watch. "We can't keep this up much longer. The yearling auction's starting in an hour and a half, and we're supposed to report early. Mr. Fairfield said—"

Just then Brigitte's door opened. Frank nudged Joe, and the two of them slipped farther back into the nook.

A second later Brigitte emerged, wearing a white suit. She was engrossed in a French magazine and didn't even glance up as she closed her door and headed for the elevator bank.

When the elevator had come and gone, Joe rushed over to her door. He reached into the pocket of his jeans and pulled out a lock-picking kit. "Don't leave home without it," he called out cheerfully to Frank.

"Yeah, yeah, yeah," Frank muttered. "Just open the door. In case you hadn't noticed, we're in a busy hotel. If someone sees, we'll have a lot of explaining to do."

Joe had the lock picked in less than a minute. He pushed open the door and stepped inside. Brigitte's room was enormous and luxurious: antique furniture, oriental rugs, and stained glass windows. There were vases of long-stemmed roses everywhere, filling the air with their heady scent. He remembered that Brigitte was some sort of a rich entrepreneur. She would have to be to afford a place like this, he thought.

Joe rubbed his hands together briskly and looked around. "I'll start with her closet."

"I'll take her desk and dresser," Frank offered. "And let's be quick about this, okay? We have no idea how long she'll be gone."

"She's probably headed over to Fairfield, Inc., to preview more yearlings before the auction," Joe said as he opened her closet door. "I bet she won't be back for the rest of the afternoon."

Brigitte's closet was filled with dozens of outfits. Joe couldn't believe it. "You'd think she was here for the whole summer instead of a few days," he said to Frank.

"Hey, here's something," Frank called out over his shoulder. He was standing over Brigitte's desk. "It's a fax of an article from some German newspaper. And it's got a picture of Prince Zafir in it."

"That's weird," Joe said with a frown. "Can you figure out what it says?"

"I only took a year of German," Frank replied. "I don't know if I can read it or not. Maybe I can get the gist of it."

As he waited for Frank to translate the article, Joe went through all of Brigitte's clothes and searched through their pockets. All he came up with was some change and a book of matches from a restaurant called Marlene's in Munich, Germany.

And then he hit the jackpot. His fingers fell upon a white silk blouse with a missing button. Joe studied the other buttons closely. They were small and silver-colored, with an etched leaf design on each.

"Hey, Frank!" Joe said excitedly. "Check this out! I've found a shirt with a missing—"

He stopped suddenly. His ears were picking up a distinctly unwelcome sound: the sound of a key in the lock. Brigitte was back, and she was about to discover the two of them in her room!

Chapter
Sixteen

NANCY WALKED into her hotel room and found George sitting by the window, reading a book.

George set her book aside and rose to her feet. "Where have you been? And why do you look so pale?" she demanded.

Nancy flopped down on her bed. "It's a long story," she replied wearily. "The punch line is, someone slipped some arsenic into my bottled water. I think it might have been Eileen's brother Sean."

"What?" George cried out. "I don't understand. Why would he do a thing like that? Have you seen a doctor? Are you—"

"I'm okay," Nancy cut in, smiling weakly. "A doctor gave me some medicine, and I feel a lot

164

better. I took a cab from the clinic. The thing is, I need to find Sean right away. Can you help me?"

George crossed her arms and gazed at her friend skeptically. "What did the doctor say? You're probably supposed to spend the day in bed, right?"

"Something like that," Nancy admitted. "I promise I'll take it easy and let you do all the major legwork. And after we're done, I'll come straight back here, hop into bed, and sleep for twenty-four hours."

"Okay," George said uncertainly. "But if you have a relapse, we're coming back here immediately."

Ten minutes later Nancy and George were out the door. They took a cab and picked up the rental car at the spa parking lot.

Then after looking up Sean's address in the phone book, they tried his house, but no one was home. Next, they drove to his office, where they spoke to one of his assistants.

"Dr. O'Neill got a call to go out to Addison Farms about an hour ago," she told Nancy and George. "You might try there. And after that he's due at the Fairfield Yearling Auction."

The two girls got back in the car and headed out to the Addison farm. When they arrived, Nancy pointed to the side of the long driveway, which was overgrown with honeysuckle bushes. "Pull over there," she instructed George. "I don't want to announce our visit."

"So what's the plan?" George asked Nancy as she parked the car. "If Sean is here, are you going to ask him point-blank about the arsenic and hope he confesses?"

Nancy shook her head. "I think I'll try the indirect approach. First, I'll ask him about Katie My Love and Pat on the Back. Then I'll try to find out if he made up that story about Jimmy wanting to borrow a hundred dollars. Now that Tracy's confessed everything, Sean is the only one who still maintains that Jimmy has a gambling problem."

Nancy and George walked toward the house. It was late in the afternoon, but the August sun made it feel like high noon. Nancy wiped a bead of sweat off her forehead; the heat was draining her of what little energy she had. Hang in there, Drew, she told herself. This is an important lead, and it can't wait another day.

They reached the house and rang the doorbell. No one answered. Nancy noted that there were no cars in the driveway except for a battered old pickup truck.

Nancy glanced at her watch. "The yearling auction is starting in an hour," she murmured. "Maybe everyone's over there."

George held up the car keys. "You want to head over there, then?" she asked Nancy.

"I guess so—" Nancy began. But then something caught her eye.

Off in the distance, Mr. Addison was walking

across a large field, away from his house and barns. He was dressed in a red shirt, jeans, and work boots, and was looking around furtively.

"I wonder what he's up to?" Nancy said.

George cupped her hand over her eyes, shielding them from the afternoon sun. "Is that Mr. Addison?" she said after a moment.

"Yup," Nancy replied. "He's going somewhere, and he's acting as though he doesn't want to be followed, which is exactly what we're going to do." She grabbed George's arm. "Come on! If we don't hurry, we'll lose sight of him."

"But I thought we were looking for Sean," George pointed out.

"Maybe Mr. Addison is meeting him somewhere," Nancy told her. "Let's go!"

Nancy and George made their way across the field, making sure to stay out of Mr. Addison's line of vision by hiding behind barns and trees. Mr. Addison was walking toward what appeared to be the far edge of his property. It was humid outside, and the trek was tiring for Nancy. She paused occasionally to catch her breath and wipe the sweat from her brow.

Mr. Addison finally stopped walking when he came to a dilapidated barn that was standing alone in the middle of a small, overgrown pasture at the edge of some woods. He took one last peek over his shoulder, fiddled with what appeared to be a lock on the door, and went inside.

Nancy and George hid behind a hedge of

raspberry bushes about twenty-five yards away. Nancy was glad that they were both wearing neutral colors. "I wonder what he's doing in there?" she whispered.

George shrugged. "Your guess is as good as mine."

The two of them waited in silence. Their legs were scratched from wading through the overgrown pasture, and the heat was unrelenting. Nancy struggled to fight the fatigue that was overtaking her body. Just a little while longer, she told herself.

Five minutes later Mr. Addison emerged from the barn, locked it, and headed in the direction of the house. Nancy gestured for George to bend down behind the hedge. Mr. Addison went past them without even glancing in their direction.

When he was totally out of sight, Nancy stood up. "Let's check out that barn," she told George.

George nodded. "Definitely. I'm really curious now."

After making sure Mr. Addison wasn't doubling back, Nancy and George hurried over to the barn. Once there, Nancy pressed her ear to the door. All she could hear was the steady droning of the cicadas in the trees. There were no sounds coming from inside.

"Huh," Nancy murmured. "I wonder what the deal is?"

Then she spotted something on the ground

near the door. It was a purple watch with a cartoon cat on it. The watch face was cracked, and the band was covered with mud.

Nancy picked it up. "This is Jimmy's," she said slowly. "He was wearing it that morning at the track."

George's eyes widened. "You mean—"

"I mean he must be in here. There's no other explanation." Nancy banged on the barn door. "Hello? Jimmy, are you in there?" she shouted loudly.

There was no reply. Nancy reached into her shoulder bag and took out her lock-picking kit, then began working on the padlock.

It took a while, but finally the lock popped open. Then she opened the door and rushed into the barn.

Jimmy was there, sitting in a rickety-looking chair in the back of the barn. His arms and feet were bound, his eyes were blindfolded, and there was a gag over his mouth. His hair and clothes were disheveled and dirty.

"Jimmy!" Nancy cried out. She ran over to him and untied his blindfold and gag.

Jimmy blinked at Nancy, then at George. He seemed to be completely disoriented.

"Jimmy?" George said softly. "Do you recognize us? It's George Fayne and Nancy Drew, Eileen's friends."

Jimmy shook his head briskly, as though clearing the cobwebs. "I'm sorry," he murmured, his voice ragged and hoarse. "It's just that it's been so long since I've seen daylight."

Nancy continued untying his bonds. "What happened to you, Jimmy?"

"Am I at Addison Farms?" Jimmy asked her suddenly.

"You're in some barn way at the edge of Mr. Addison's property," Nancy told him. "We just saw him come and go a few minutes ago. I think he's on his way to the yearling auction now."

Jimmy's eyes flashed angrily. "Just as I thought. Abe and Sean *were* behind this!"

So I was right about Sean being up to no good, Nancy thought. "They kidnapped you and brought you here?" she asked him.

"I didn't actually see my kidnappers," Jimmy replied, rubbing his wrists gingerly. "But I'm sure it had to be them. You see, I was in the middle of working on a story about the yearling auction when I stumbled upon something really big. All the signs pointed to a huge conspiracy between Sean and Abe. I'm sure that's why they did this—to keep me from investigating further and to shut me up."

"A conspiracy?" Nancy repeated, puzzled. "What kind of conspiracy?"

"I was just beginning to scratch the surface," Jimmy said grimly. "But it looked as though—"

Just then Nancy heard a noise. She held her

finger to her lips. Jimmy fell silent. Nancy glanced around just in time to see a flash of red in the doorway. Then the door slammed shut.

Nancy got to her feet, ran to the door, and tried to open it. It was locked.

George and Jimmy crept up behind her. "What's going on?" George whispered anxiously. "Is someone out there?"

"I think it's Mr. Addison," Nancy whispered back. "He must have seen our car in the driveway!"

Nancy pressed her ear to the door. She could hear Mr. Addison moving through the tall weeds surrounding the barn. What was he up to? she wondered. Did he plan to trap the three of them in here indefinitely? But sooner or later they would be able to get out, and they would go straight to the authorities.

Suddenly Nancy smelled something strange. She sniffed the air, trying to identify it. She felt a shiver of fear when she realized what it was.

She turned to George and Jimmy. "It's smoke," she said quickly. "Mr. Addison's set the barn on fire."

Frank's face was pressed up against a fuzzy robe. At least he *thought* it was a robe. It was impossible to tell, since the inside of Brigitte Bouvier's closet was pitch-black.

He moved his hand around, trying to find a

less congested spot to stand in. He touched something silky, then something velvety, then something that didn't feel like a piece of clothing.

"Hey, stop poking me in the stomach!" Joe whispered.

"Oh, sorry," Frank whispered back.

Frank heard Joe shifting around slightly. "I can't move with all the suitcases stacked up in here," Joe complained.

"These are definitely not ideal working conditions," Frank agreed.

"Hey, bro?" Joe said. "What are we going to do if Brigitte decides she doesn't like what she's wearing?"

"Improvise like mad," Frank replied grimly. Just then he heard a sound. "Shh. I think she's coming out of the bathroom."

Through the closet door Frank could make out the sound of Brigitte entering the room. She opened a drawer, then closed it. Then she sat down on her bed—there was a faint squeaking of bedsprings—and riffled through some papers.

All of a sudden Frank had the overpowering urge to sneeze. He sucked in a breath and put a finger between his upper lip and nose. No sneezing, he willed himself. No sneezing. No sneezing.

The urge subsided. Relieved, Frank let his breath out in a whoosh. But just then he heard Brigitte's footsteps again.

Frank froze. Unless he was mistaken, it sounded as though Brigitte was heading for the closet.

The footsteps stopped. Frank heard the doorknob turn, and he scrunched back instinctively toward the rear of the closet. He saw a sliver of light as the door began to open . . .

At that moment the phone rang. The door closed, and the footsteps moved away.

"Saved by the bell," Joe whispered.

"Shh!" Frank hissed.

Brigitte picked up the phone. "Hello?" She paused, then said, "*Ja, ja*, this is Berthe. I have been waiting for your call."

Frank frowned. Why was Brigitte calling herself Berthe? he wondered. He also noticed that her English sounded very different suddenly. It was German-accented English, not the French-accented English she'd been speaking for the past few days.

There was a long silence. Brigitte seemed to be listening to the person on the other end. "I am very sorry you had to read about that in the newspaper, Ahmed," Brigitte said after a moment. "He moved at the last minute. You must understand that."

"Frank?" Joe whispered. "Are you listening to this?"

"Shh," Frank whispered back. "Of course I'm listening."

"Leave everything to me," Brigitte went on coolly. There was the snap of a cartridge being inserted into a gun. "In a few hours nothing will stand in your way. You and your group will be able to assume control of Morocco."

Chapter

Seventeen

NANCY TRIED to keep her panic at bay. The old barn was quickly going up in smoke, and she had to do something—*fast*. At the same time, due to the aftereffects of the arsenic poisoning, her body felt sluggish, and her head was spinning.

She pulled a scarf out of her shoulder bag and put it over her mouth and nose. The smoke was getting thick now, and her eyes were burning. How much longer could they last in here? The brittle wood of the barn was dry as tinder. "Stay low, guys," she told George and Jimmy. "And put something over your mouth and nose."

Jimmy took his blazer off, ripped the lining out of it, and offered half of it to George. "Thanks," she told him gratefully.

"Maybe we should make a run for it through the fire," Jimmy suggested.

Nancy assessed the situation. One of the walls was in flames; the other three were still intact. "Too dangerous," she told Jimmy. "I think our best bet is to get an ax or something and rip through one of the walls that *isn't* on fire."

"Ax, ax, ax," George repeated, glancing around. "Where's an ax when you need one?"

Nancy scanned the interior of the large barn. The floor was covered with a layer of soggy-looking hay. In the corner, she noticed a stack of firewood, plus some half-opened bags of weed killer and a rusty wheelbarrow.

Nancy's eyes returned to the woodpile. Where there was wood, there was often an ax. She moved quickly toward the woodpile and immediately noticed a faded red handle poking out of the back of it. That could be it, she thought excitedly.

Then she saw an oilcan on the ground near the woodpile. The edge of the fire was only ten feet away from it. She had to get to the woodpile before the fire spread to the oilcan!

Nancy ran to the woodpile and tugged at the red handle. It wouldn't budge.

Jimmy and George hurried up behind her. "What do you want us to do?" George asked her.

"Get that oilcan as far away from the fire as possible," Nancy said. "Jimmy, help me move some of this wood so I can free this thing up. I think it might be an ax."

It was hard for Nancy to see what she was doing. Her eyes were stinging from the smoke. But finally, she and Jimmy managed to move enough pieces of wood to loosen the red-handled object from the woodpile.

Nancy lifted it in the air. "It *is* an ax," she said triumphantly.

George took it from her. "Here, allow me. You're supposed to take it easy, remember?"

"Be my guest," Nancy told her.

George began whacking at the nearest wall. The brittle wood splintered easily. Jimmy stood nearby and kicked at the wall, trying to speed things up.

As George and Jimmy worked, Nancy eyed the oilcan nervously. Even though George had moved it to a far corner of the barn, the fire was spreading fast—it would reach the can in a matter of minutes!

"Nancy, look out!" Jimmy shouted suddenly.

Nancy glanced up. A smoldering beam was about to collapse. Reacting instinctively, she dove to the left and rolled several times. The beam came crashing down, missing her by inches.

Nancy leapt to her feet and rushed away from the beam. The flames from it were rapidly spreading. Soon the whole place would be on fire.

"The wall is down!" George called out. "Come on, guys!"

Nancy scrambled to the opening in the wall. George climbed out first, then Jimmy and Nancy followed. The three of them ran as fast as they could from the burning barn.

Seconds later Nancy heard an explosion behind her. She stopped and turned around. The barn was a blazing inferno. Flames crackled everywhere, and pillars of smoke rose into the air.

"We'd better call the fire department before this fire spreads more," Nancy said breathlessly.

"We also have to get the police and Popeye Lopez, then head over to the yearling auction," Jimmy added.

Nancy looked at him curiously. "Why Popeye Lopez?"

"I'll explain on the way," Jimmy said. "Come on—before it's too late."

As Joe continued to listen to Brigitte's conversation with Ahmed, he grew more and more incredulous. Brigitte was not a rich Parisian with a passion for horses. She was a gun-toting German named Berthe, and she appeared to be involved with a group wanting to take control of Morocco.

"I will be back in Berlin in twenty-four hours," Brigitte was saying to Ahmed. "I will expect the second half of my payment wired to my Swiss bank account by then."

Payment for what? Joe wondered.

As Brigitte wrapped up her conversation, Joe moved to the front of the closet.

"What are you doing?" Frank whispered.

"I'm going to confront Brigitte, or Berthe, or whatever her name is," Joe whispered back.

"Uh, Joe? She's got a gun," Frank pointed out. "And I'm sure she'll have no problem using it on us, especially when she finds out we've been eavesdropping on her little chat with Ahmed."

Joe frowned. His brother was right. If only Joe could see where Brigitte was standing, he might be able to take her by surprise and wrestle the gun away from her. But he couldn't see Brigitte from the closet. He and Frank would just have to stay put until Brigitte left the room.

If she left the room, Joe thought. He remembered that Brigitte had been on her way to the closet when the phone rang. What if she came back? he wondered.

Brigitte hung up a moment later. Joe listened apprehensively. What would her next move be? He tensed every muscle in his body, prepared to jump her if necessary.

But she seemed to have forgotten about whatever it was she'd wanted in the closet. Seconds later, Joe heard Brigitte walk across the room and then heard the sound of the door closing.

"Stay put," Frank said quickly. "Let's wait another minute and make sure she didn't forget something."

Joe shifted restlessly as he counted down from sixty. Brigitte didn't return. When Joe hit zero, he practically burst out of the closet.

He glanced around the room. Everything looked as it had before.

Then he turned to face his brother. "What do you think Brigitte is up to?"

"If I didn't know better, I'd say that she's an assassin and that she's working for someone named Ahmed who wants Prince Zafir dead," Frank replied grimly. "What did she say to Ahmed? 'I am very sorry you had to read about that in the newspaper. He moved at the last minute.'"

"She could have been talking about what happened at the polo match," Joe said, nodding.

"And what else did she say? 'In a few hours, nothing will stand in your way. You and your group will be able to assume control of Morocco,'" Frank went on. "Translation: Brigitte is planning another attempt on the prince's life. Well, the yearling auction's the logical place for that, and it starts in twenty-five minutes."

"If Mr. Fairfield's estimates are right, there are going to be a thousand people there," Joe said with concern. "A thousand people—plus one maniac with a gun."

Frank went over to Brigitte's nightstand,

picked up the phone, and began dialing. "I want to alert Mr. Fairfield," he told Joe. Then he frowned and hung up. "Busy. Come on, let's go."

The Hardys left Brigitte's room, exited the hotel, and raced to the parking lot. Five minutes later, they were driving down Broadway, heading out to the Fairfield paddocks.

The traffic was heavy, which made Joe crazy. His knuckles were white as he clenched the steering wheel. "I hope we can get there in time," he murmured.

"Just stay cool," Frank told him. "We'll get there, find Prince Zafir, and get him to a safe place. And if we're very lucky, this whole thing will have been a false alarm."

Joe saw a yellow traffic light just ahead and put his foot on the accelerator. He made it just as the light turned red. "Maybe we should call the cops and have Brigitte arrested," he suggested.

"On what charges?" Frank countered. "We didn't actually hear her say she was going to kill Prince Zafir. We didn't see her with a gun, and even if we did, she might have a license to carry one. And it's not a crime to call yourself Berthe."

"Hey, I just thought of something," Joe said suddenly. "Do you think she had anything to do with Marco's murder?"

"It's possible," Frank replied. "There's the poison dart business, too."

"She must have faked the attack on herself at the raceway—probably to throw suspicion off her." Joe muttered. "I can't believe she had us all duped!"

Ten minutes later the Hardys arrived at Fairfield, Inc. The parking lot was full, so Joe parked in an illegal spot on the street. Then he and Frank rushed into the auction pavilion.

Inside, it was a zoo. Every seat seemed to be filled. Down front, below the seats, was a stage where the yearlings would be paraded around while the bidding took place. The auctioneer, a silver-haired man wearing a black tuxedo, was standing at the podium, shuffling through his notes.

The auctioneer tapped on the microphone. "Ladies and gentlemen," he said, "the auction is about to start. Please remember that credit extended at previous auctions does not apply to this auction. If you have not done so already, please go to our credit office and open an account. Please also be reminded that title passes to the final bidder at the fall of the hammer. At that time the final bidder will assume all responsibility for the horse." He added, "The conditions of the sale are listed on page thirteen of your catalogs. Please review this information carefully."

Frank and Joe went halfway down the aisle, toward the stage. "Do you see Prince Zafir or Brigitte?" Frank asked Joe.

Joe glanced around. "No," he said after a moment. "We're going to have to split up and look around. In the meantime, we should try to track down Mr. Fairfield."

"Are you looking for me?"

Joe turned around. Mr. Fairfield was coming down the aisle, holding a clipboard in his hands. He was dressed in a gray suit, and he seemed tense and harried.

"Just the man we want," Joe said. "We have a major crisis on our hands."

Mr. Fairfield raised his eyebrows. "Crisis? That's not something I need to hear right now. Can it wait?"

"No, it can't wait," Frank replied. He lowered his voice and added, "There's a possibility that Brigitte Bouvier is going to make an assassination attempt on Prince Zafir at this auction."

"What!" Mr. Fairfield burst out. Then he shook his head quickly. "Wait a second—not here. Come with me."

He led the Hardys to a secluded spot in the back of the pavilion. "All right," he said quietly. "Now, tell me what on earth you're talking about."

Joe explained about the ticket stub in Brigitte's purse, the missing silver button, and her phone conversation with the man named Ahmed. When he'd finished, Mr. Fairfield looked totally bewildered. "Ms. Bouvier is a personal friend of one of our board of directors. I simply can't believe what you're telling me."

"Well, believe it," Joe told him.

Just then the auctioneer banged his hammer on the podium. "If the bid spotters will please take their places, we will begin the auction," he said loudly. "Our first horse, Hip Number One, is a bay filly out of Emma Pink by Midnight Star." Behind him, a young guy dressed in a tuxedo led a slender brown yearling onto the stage. She trotted about confidently, apparently unfazed by the crowd and the spotlights.

Several other young men dressed in tuxedos appeared at the bottom of the aisles. Joe figured they must be the bid spotters.

"I don't want the crowd in a panic about this business," Mr. Fairfield said to the Hardys. "And I don't want to confront Ms. Bouvier without more proof. I think the only solution is for you to find the prince and get him off the premises as quickly as possible."

"Do you have any idea where he might be sitting?" Frank asked him.

Mr. Fairfield pulled his cellular phone out of his pocket and punched in some numbers. "Margo Olson is in charge of seat assignments," he murmured. After a moment he shook his head and hung up. "She's not answering. I'm afraid you'll have to search all the seats."

Then his eyes wandered past Joe and fixed on someone in the distance. "Noah," he called out, crooking his finger. "Can you come here, please? I need to talk to you."

Joe turned around. A tall blond guy dressed in jeans and a black linen shirt was standing near one of the doors. That must be Jimmy English's roommate, Joe thought.

Noah came over, barely glancing at Frank and Joe. "Isn't this a peculiar time for a father-son chat?" he asked Mr. Fairfield dryly.

"This is Frank and Joe Hardy," Mr. Fairfield said, ignoring his son's comment. "We need your help looking for Prince Zafir and Brigitte Bouvier. I can't go into it, except to say that it's vital we find them."

Noah looked puzzled, but he seemed to comprehend the urgency in his father's voice. "No problem," he said. He turned to Frank and Joe. "I guess I'll take this section?"

"Great," Frank replied. "I'll take the center section. Joe, you take the far left."

Joe nodded, then went into action. The auction was in full swing; the auctioneer was getting bids for the brown horse that was Hip Number One. "Do I hear ten thousand? I've got ten thousand in the corner. How about ten thousand and five? Ten thousand and five going once, going twice . . ." Above him, a huge, lighted scoreboard kept track of the bids.

Joe reached the far left section of the pavilion and started down one of the aisles. He scanned the sea of faces all around him. No Prince Zafir, and no Brigitte Bouvier.

Joe reached up to scratch his head. Just then the auctioneer said, "And we have ten thousand five from the young gentleman in the aisle."

Joe froze. The guy was looking straight at him. "Uh, no," Joe said quickly. "I was just— Anyway, cancel the bid. I'm sorry, my apologies."

The auctioneer frowned at him, then continued with the bidding. Hip Number One was sold a minute later for seventeen thousand dollars.

Soon Hip Number Two was led out onto the stage. He was very familiar to Joe.

"And now we have one of the great highlights of our evening," the auctioneer said. The crowd began buzzing excitedly. "This is Goldenrod, out of Golden Folly by Lightning Rod. As many of you know, this colt is the one and only foal of Golden Folly, who died while giving birth to him. He is destined to become a star in the racing world, just as Golden Folly was. . . ."

Joe started up another aisle. Suddenly, he felt optimistic. He realized that Prince Zafir was bound to bid on Goldenrod, so Joe should be able to spot him. Excellent, he thought.

Then Joe realized something else—something that wasn't so excellent. If he could spot the prince, so could Brigitte Bouvier.

"Do I hear a hundred thousand for Goldenrod?" the auctioneer said.

The crowd was in a fever pitch. Luke Ventura,

who was sitting in the center section, raised his hand.

"We have a hundred thousand," the auctioneer announced. "Do I hear two hundred thousand?"

"Stop the auction!"

Joe's head shot up. Nancy, George, a tall guy with glasses, and a police officer had just entered the pavilion.

The tall guy came forward. "Stop the auction!" he repeated loudly. "You're all the victims of a huge scam. That horse isn't Goldenrod!"

Chapter

Eighteen

NANCY HEARD a collective gasp from the audience. Then everyone began talking at once.

Amidst all the chaos and confusion, Nancy glanced down and noticed Joe staring up at her. For that matter, so were Frank and Noah. Nancy wondered what the three guys were up to; besides the bid spotters, they were the only ones standing in the aisles.

Mr. Fairfield walked to the podium and spoke into the microphone. He looked tense. "I'm sorry for the interruption, ladies and gentlemen," he said. "We'll have it taken care of in just one minute, and then we can resume the auction—"

"This is going to take longer than a minute,

Mr. Fairfield," Jimmy cut in. The whole pavilion was silent, hanging on his every word.

"You see, the real foal of Golden Folly and Lightning Rod died at birth along with its dam," the young reporter went on. "The yearling on-stage is the foal of Katie My Love and Pat on the Back, born only two hours later. Abe Addison and Dr. Sean O'Neill, who delivered both foals, conspired to switch them and keep the whole thing a secret. Mr. Addison couldn't bear to lose all the money he knew Golden Folly's foal would bring."

Abe Addison, who was sitting in one of the upper rows, jumped to his feet. His face was beet red. "That's a lie!" he shouted. "Don't listen to this guy! He's just a hack reporter trying to stir up trouble!"

Sean, who was sitting next to him, stood up as well. He put his hand on Mr. Addison's arm, as though trying to subdue him. "Clearly, there's been some sort of misunderstanding," he said affably to Jimmy. "And this isn't the time or the place to discuss it."

"This is definitely the time and the place to discuss it—before someone gets suckered into buying an inferior horse for millions of dollars," Jimmy retorted.

Mr. Fairfield came rushing up the aisle, his arms held stiffly at his sides. "I don't know what you think you're doing, bringing in the police and disrupting my auction like this," he said to Jimmy in a quiet, angry voice. "You're making some very serious allegations. Do you have any proof to back up what you're saying?"

"We have a witness who'll back up everything Jimmy's saying," Nancy declared. "I'll be right back." She disappeared through the entrance door, then returned a few moments later with Popeye Lopez. He glanced around the pavilion nervously; when his beady eyes fell on Abe Addison and Sean O'Neill, he turned several shades paler.

"Popeye was working as a stablehand at Addison Farms last year," Nancy explained to Mr. Fairfield. "He saw Golden Folly's real foal die. He knew something funny was up when Mr. Addison announced to the press the next morning that Goldenrod was alive and well and that Katie My Love and Pat on the Back's foal had died instead. When he asked Mr. Addison about it, Mr. Addison told him to keep his mouth shut, or he'd find himself at the bottom of Saratoga Lake."

Mr. Fairfield frowned. He glanced at Mr. Addison and Sean, then at Nancy again. "Go on," he said grimly.

"Popeye promised he'd keep quiet," Nancy continued. "He was scared for his life. A month later he quit his job and went into business for himself."

Jimmy took up the story. "About two weeks

ago, when I was researching my story about the auction, I decided to interview Popeye. I knew he'd worked as a stablehand at Addison Farms around the time of Goldenrod's birth, and I thought he might have some good stories. At first he refused to talk to me. In fact, he acted so nervous that I got suspicious. Then he let slip something that made me even more suspicious—something about not being able to save Goldenrod."

"Jimmy asked Sean O'Neill what the big mystery was with Goldenrod's birth," George announced. "Sean is his fiancée's brother, so Jimmy figured he could get the real story. But Sean acted as though there wasn't any mystery. Then the next night—three nights ago—someone sneaked up on Jimmy in the *Sentinel* parking lot, knocked him out, and kidnapped him."

"Jimmy didn't see them, but it was Sean and Abe," Nancy said. "George and I found Jimmy tied up in a barn on Mr. Addison's property this afternoon. When we tried to free him, Mr. Addison locked us in the barn and set fire to it."

"That is a bald-faced lie!" Mr. Addison shouted, shaking his fist. "I'll sue you all for slander! I'll—"

The police officer stepped forward. "I'm sorry, Mr. Addison, but we'll have to take you in for questioning. You, too, Dr. O'Neill."

As Mr. Addison continued to protest, Nancy noticed that many of the people had left their seats and were crowding the aisles, trying to listen in on the confrontation between Mr. Addison, Sean O'Neill, and the others.

Then out of the corner of her eye Nancy noticed Frank coming up one of the aisles, two steps at a time. He stopped at the top of the aisle and made a motion for her to come over.

Curious, Nancy went over to him. "What's up?" she asked him in a low voice.

"Do you have a minute?" Frank said. "We have a different kind of crisis on our hands."

"What can I do?" Nancy said immediately.

"Do you know what Prince Zafir looks like? And Brigitte Bouvier?" Frank asked her.

"Sure," Nancy replied. "I saw both of them at Mr. Fairfield's party."

"Great," Frank said. "Can you help us find them? It's a long story, but the gist of it is that Brigitte is probably going to make an assassination attempt on the prince at any moment, and we have to get him out of here fast."

Nancy gasped. Brigitte Bouvier was the woman who'd found Marco Donatelli's body. And now Frank was telling her that she was an assassin.

Nancy wanted to ask a million questions, but she knew that now was not the time. "Just tell me what rows to cover," she said tersely.

Frank pointed them out to her. "The last time we saw Brigitte, she was wearing a white suit," he told her. "And, Nancy—be careful. She's carrying a gun."

Frank started down another aisle. Sean O'Neill and Mr. Addison were continuing to argue with the police officer in the back. The audience was swarming into the aisles; the place was a zoo. He wondered how he would ever find the prince or Brigitte now.

Frank reached the bottom of the aisle and then started up another. When he got halfway up, he hesitated. There were three men sitting at the end of one of the rows. They were dressed in shorts, T-shirts, and baseball caps, and their faces were hidden behind their catalogs. Because most of the people at the auction were dressed up, the three men looked out of place.

One of the men lowered his catalog for a second. He had black hair and a pencil-thin mustache.

It was Prince Zafir, Frank realized in an instant. He must have decided to come in semi-disguise because of what had happened at the polo match.

Frank jogged up to the prince and leaned down toward him. The two bodyguards immediately threw down their catalogs and reached into their pockets.

"Take it easy," Frank told them quickly, then turned to the prince. "Could you come with me?

Mr. Fairfield needs to see you right away." Frank didn't want to tell the prince about Brigitte until he was safely out of the room for fear he'd panic.

"What does he wish to see me about, Mr. Hardy?" Prince Zafir asked him. "Surely it can wait. We're in the middle of the auction, and with this trouble about Goldenrod . . ."

While the prince was talking, some instinct told Frank to look up. He felt a shiver of apprehension. Brigitte was standing in the aisle, a few rows behind the prince. She was reaching into her purse, and she had her eyes fixed on the prince.

Suddenly Brigitte's hand came out of her purse. She was holding a gun.

"Get down!" Frank shouted to the prince.

One of the bid spotters accidentally bumped into Brigitte from behind, and she whirled around, poised to shoot. It was all the distraction Frank needed. He raced up the aisle two steps at a time and tackled her to the ground before she knew what was happening.

Brigitte yelled something unintelligible, and her gun went off. The place erupted in total chaos; people began screaming and scrambling to get out of their seats. On stage, Goldenrod was whinnying in panic. Frank wondered anxiously if anyone had been shot.

Beneath him, Brigitte was struggling furiously. For a small woman, she was surprisingly strong. "You'd better give up," Frank told her, keeping her gun arm pinned so she couldn't pull the trigger again. "We know what you're up to, and there's no way—*ow!*"

Brigitte had reached up and clawed at his eyes with her nails. Frank was momentarily blinded by the pain, and he loosened his hold on her. Brigitte took advantage of this and wriggled free of his grasp. Within seconds she was back on her feet.

Then, before Frank could stop her, Brigitte grabbed Chelsea Vaughn, who was trying to leave her seat. In one swift motion, Brigitte twisted Chelsea's arm behind her back and jammed the gun against the side of her head. Chelsea's dark eyes widened in terror. Brigitte was smiling coldly.

"No one make a move," Brigitte announced, "or I will have to shoot this pretty little girl."

Chapter

Nineteen

EVERYONE in the pavilion froze.

Frank took a deep breath. One wrong move, and Chelsea would be dead, he thought.

Mr. Vaughn, who'd been sitting next to his daughter, took his ten-gallon hat off and held it out to Brigitte. "Don't hurt her," he pleaded. The Texan, who was usually so blustery and confident, sounded totally panicked. "What do you want—money? I've got millions—heck, I've got billions. Just let my baby go, and I'll give you whatever you want."

"Thank you for your generous offer, Mr. Vaughn," Brigitte said pleasantly. "Unfortunately, I must turn you down. I plan to take your daughter for a ride."

Chelsea began crying. Brigitte rammed the gun

harder against the side of her head. "Does everyone understand what I'm saying?" she said loudly. "Chelsea and I are leaving the premises together. If anyone tries to stop us or follow us, I will have to kill her."

Frank clenched his fists, feeling helpless. What could he do? Brigitte was going to make her getaway with Chelsea as a hostage. For all he knew, the assassin was going to kill Chelsea, no matter what the outcome. She was ruthless enough to do anything.

Suddenly Frank did a double take. Just up the aisle from Brigitte there was a small flurry of movement behind the seats. His eyes widened. It was Joe, snaking along the floor. He was trying to sneak up on Brigitte!

I've got to distract Brigitte so Joe can get to her, Frank thought. "Brigitte," he said. "Why don't you let Chelsea go and take me instead?"

Brigitte arched her eyebrows at him. She looked amused. "You, Frank Hardy? I'm afraid you would make a terrible hostage. You are much too feisty, as I found to my chagrin just a minute ago. . . ."

While Brigitte talked, Frank tried to surreptitiously assess Joe's position. As far as he could see, his brother was about six feet from Brigitte.

But there was a complication. Two elderly women in the audience had spotted Joe and were staring at him. Would they give him away to Brigitte by mistake? Frank wondered anxiously.

Frank turned his attention back to Brigitte. He had to do something to stall for time and to distract the two elderly women from Joe.

"You might as well give up, Brigitte. The police have proof that you killed Marco Donatelli," Frank fibbed. "They know you were responsible for the cyanide dart, too. Why have one more murder on your head?"

For a moment Brigitte's cool demeanor slipped. Frank had definitely caught her off guard. "The police have proof?" she said incredulously. Then she shook her head quickly. "You are lying to me. The police have no proof." She narrowed her eyes at him. "If you insist on playing games with me, Mr. Hardy, I will have to shoot you, too."

Just then one of the elderly women spoke up. "Where do you suppose that young man is going, Enid?" she said to her companion.

Brigitte overheard her and whirled around. For a split second, her gun wavered away from Chelsea's head. Frank acted instantly. He reached for Brigitte's gun arm and squeezed her wrist in a bone-crunching hold. She yelped in pain but managed to keep hold of the gun. At the same moment, Joe leapt from his crouched position behind the seats and pulled Chelsea away from Brigitte, out of the line of fire.

Brigitte started to grab for Frank's throat with her free hand, but Frank intercepted her. Then he delivered a swift karate kick to her stomach. Brigitte yelled and doubled over. Frank twisted her gun arm, and her fingers fluttered open, releasing the gun. Frank caught it in midair and swiftly took the cartridge out of it. He noted that the gun was a nine-millimeter Luger—the same kind that had been used at the polo match.

The police officer who'd been questioning Mr. Addison and Sean hurried down the aisle, his own gun in hand. Frank noticed that Mr. Addison and Sean were taking advantage of the situation by trying to sneak out the door. But Nancy, George, Jimmy, and Popeye Lopez reacted immediately, stopping them before they could get away.

The police officer nodded at Frank. "I'll take over now," he said gruffly.

"Be my guest," Frank told him.

Brigitte's eyes were blazing with fury. "I will get you for this," she hissed at Frank and Joe.

"You're going to have a hard time doing that from your prison cell," Joe said cheerfully. "But look on the bright side, Brigitte or Berthe or whatever your name is. You can look us up when they let you out in eighty or ninety years."

Nancy smiled as Eileen wrapped her arms around Jimmy and kissed him for what seemed like the hundredth time. Jimmy blushed and grinned.

"I'm sorry, but I can't help myself," Eileen apologized. "I'm just so incredibly happy that you're back, safe and sound."

Nancy, Eileen, Jimmy, George, and Noah were hanging out at the Fairfield paddocks. It was Sunday morning, and they were sitting on the grass eating bagels and drinking coffee. Nearby, several horses were being washed down. Steam rose from their bodies, and they snorted and shivered with pleasure.

Nancy gazed at Eileen. Her friend was in such a good mood that she hated to break the news to her about Sean.

The night before, when Jimmy, Nancy, and George had shown up at Eileen's door, they'd told her only half the story—that Mr. Addison had been behind the kidnapping. Jimmy had wanted to save the part about Sean for later, to spare her feelings. They also hadn't told her about Mr. Addison setting the barn on fire, nearly killing the three of them.

Eileen ruffled Jimmy's blond hair. "Are you *sure* you're okay, sweetie? That awful Mr. Addison didn't rough you up or anything?"

"Well, not exactly," Jimmy replied slowly. He glanced at Nancy, then at Eileen again. "I guess it's time we let you in on the whole story, Eileen."

Eileen frowned. "The whole story? What are you talking about?"

Jimmy took a deep breath, then told her everything, beginning with Goldenrod's birth and ending with the events at the yearling auction. Eileen was trembling by the time he was finished.

"No," she murmured, shaking her head. "That can't be. There's no way my brother could have done all those things!"

George put her hand on Eileen's arm. "I'm sorry, but it's all true," she said gently. "After Jimmy asked Sean about Goldenrod's birth on Tuesday night, Sean went straight to Mr. Addison and told him what was going on. Mr. Addison was terrified that Jimmy would get to the bottom of their scheme and suggested that they kill him right away. But Sean talked him out of it—for your sake, Eileen."

Jimmy took up the story. "So Sean and Mr. Addison decided to kidnap me instead. Their plan was to keep their identities totally secret while they kept me prisoner. They did a pretty good job of it, too. They had me blindfolded the entire time, and they never talked to me, even when they fed me and stuff."

"Then," Nancy went on, "once Goldenrod was sold at the auction and Mr. Addison and Sean had the money in their pockets, they were going to let Jimmy go and leave town. They confessed all this to the police last night." She added, "Sean also confessed to breaking into our hotel room and leaving the knife and note, making the threatening phone call, trying to push me over the bridge, and slipping the arsenic into my bottled water yesterday. He was trying to keep me from finding Jimmy."

"Even though they decided to spare *my* life," Jimmy said grimly, "Mr. Addison and Sean would have had no problems killing Nancy if she'd gotten too close to solving the mystery."

Eileen gazed down at the ground, still shaking her head. "This is like a nightmare," she whispered. "Fraud, kidnapping, setting barns on fire, break-ins, arsenic poisoning . . ."

Noah was just about to take a sip of his coffee. But when he heard the phrase "arsenic poisoning," he stopped and stared at his coffee for a second. Then he shrugged and resumed drinking it.

"I talked to my father this morning," he said to Eileen. "He's pretty sick about the whole thing, too. Apparently, everyone bought the yearling switch because Goldenrod—well, the horse everyone *knows* as Goldenrod, anyway— looks kind of like Golden Folly, with the same coloring and markings and everything. And even though his genes aren't so hot, his form is really good."

"Popeye Lopez," Eileen said suddenly. "Didn't he have something to do with all this?"

Jimmy explained Popeye's role in the whole story. "He's going to testify against Mr. Addison and your brother," he finished. "After we made it out of that burning barn yesterday, we found Popeye at the Palomino Grill. I convinced him to talk to the authorities. With the kidnapping and attempted murder charges, Mr. Addison and Sean were going to go to jail, anyway, so there was no way they could hurt Popeye."

"They'd threatened to kill Popeye if he talked," Nancy explained. "That's why Popeye acted so afraid when I confronted him at the track."

Eileen turned to Jimmy. Tears were brimming in her eyes. "I don't know what to say," she murmured brokenly. "I'm in total shock about Sean. After everything that's happened, you probably want to postpone the wedding."

Jimmy put his arm around her. "Absolutely not," he told her softly. "We're getting married Thanksgiving weekend, and that's all there is to it."

"Free breakfast? Hey, why didn't anyone invite us?"

Nancy glanced up. Joe was heading their way, followed by Frank.

"Hi, guys!" she called out with a smile. Frank sat down beside her. "Hi, yourself. You look pretty beautiful for someone who was poisoned just yesterday."

Nancy blushed. "I'm totally cured, thanks to a good night's rest and another trip to the doctor," she told him.

"You two know each other?" Noah asked Nancy.

Nancy thought she detected a hint of jealousy

in Noah's voice. "Um, yes," she replied. "Frank, Joe, and I go way back." She turned to the Hardys. "Where have you guys been? I tried to call you at your hotel this morning."

"We've been hanging out with Sergeant Aiello and our other buddies down at headquarters," Joe explained. "We wanted to get the whole story on Brigitte."

"And? What *is* the whole story on Brigitte?" George asked.

Joe reached into a white paper bag that was lying on the grass and pulled out an onion bagel. "Her real name is Berthe Lindgren," he said between bites. "She's a professional assassin wanted by the CIA, Interpol, the Mossad—you name it. She was hired by political enemies of Prince Zafir to eliminate him without drawing any attention or suspicion to themselves."

"That's why Berthe came up with the plan to kill him here in Saratoga," Frank declared. "She knew he would be making one of his rare trips abroad to attend the auction. She got the idea to pose as a rich Parisian named Brigitte Bouvier who was interested in Goldenrod."

"She even managed to butter up one of Fairfield, Inc.'s board of directors at a party in Paris last month," Joe added. "That's why Mr. Fairfield had to treat her like a VIP. He thought she was a close personal friend of the guy."

"But Berthe didn't count on a major glitch,"

Frank continued. "Marco Donatelli. She'd met him in Rome years ago, when she lived there under the alias Alessandra Casale. He recognized her at Mr. Fairfield's party and asked her why she was running around with a phony name. She tried to tell him he was mistaken, that she wasn't Alessandra Casale, but he wouldn't buy it."

Joe grabbed George's cup of coffee and took a sip. "Do you mind? Thanks. Anyway, that was the argument I saw Berthe and Marco having outside the dance tent. Later Berthe decided that Marco had to be eliminated. She was afraid of having her cover blown, plus the whole mission, too. She arranged to meet him privately at the rose garden—"

"And that was the end of Marco Donatelli," Frank finished.

Nancy frowned. "But what about the cyanide dart business? And the incident at the track? Was she behind them, too?"

Frank nodded. "After murdering Marco, she knew she had to divert suspicion from herself. So she came up with a plan to make it look as though someone was targeting all the potential buyers of Goldenrod." He added, "She staged phony murder attempts against Mr. Vaughn and herself. In the case of Mr. Vaughn, she missed him and hit Goldenrod instead."

"Her aim wasn't so great at the polo match, either," Joe remarked. "She tried to shoot Prince

Zafir from the parking lot, but he moved at the last minute, so she hit his champagne glass instead."

"We started getting suspicious of her," Frank continued, "so we got the idea to hide in her closet the next day—"

"*We* got the idea?" Joe interrupted. "Excuse me?"

Frank grinned. "Okay, *Joe* got the idea. Anyway, you guys know the rest of the story."

"Speaking of champagne glasses . . ." Jimmy gazed affectionately at Eileen. "We have a wedding to plan. What do you say we go back to your apartment and start making some calls?"

Eileen hugged him. "Definitely!"

Jimmy kissed her on the cheek, then smiled at everyone in the group. "I hope you're all free the Saturday after Thanksgiving. It wouldn't be a wedding without you."

"I'm free," Noah said cheerfully, then put his arm around Nancy. "You'll come as my date, right? I'll fly you in from River Heights in my dad's private jet, and I'll rent a limo to take us to the wedding, and—"

Nancy stared at him and laughed. "You really don't give up, do you?"

Epilogue

Three months later . . .

I NOW PRONOUNCE you husband and wife. You
may kiss the bride."

The minister smiled as Jimmy took Eileen in
his arms and gave her a long, passionate kiss.
The whole room broke into cheers and clapping.

George leaned toward Nancy. "Wasn't that a
totally romantic ceremony?" she whispered.

Nancy nodded. "I especially loved the vows
Jimmy and Eileen wrote."

The string quartet began playing the reces-
sional music, and Jimmy and Eileen came down
the aisle, arm in arm. Nancy thought they made
a great-looking couple. Jimmy had on a black

tuxedo with a burgundy cummerbund and bow tie, and Eileen was wearing a lacy white cocktail dress from the 1920s, a string of pearls, and a big, floppy hat. She was carrying a bouquet of daisies.

The room, one of the parlors in the Algonquin Hotel, was packed with people. Nancy glanced around. She saw the Hardys, Noah, Mr. Fairfield, Wyatt Vaughn, and Chelsea among the guests. Luke Ventura, who was George's date, wasn't there yet. He was in New York City to promote his new movie and had arranged to meet her at the reception.

Nancy and George rose from their seats to go through the receiving line. When they reached Eileen, she gave both girls a big, tearful hug. "I'm so happy, I can't stand it," she murmured.

"We're so happy you're happy," George told her with a grin. Then her expression turned serious. "Eileen, have you talked to your brother?"

Eileen shook her head. "No, and I don't know if I ever will. I can't forgive Sean for what he did to Jimmy—and to me. Right now I don't care if he rots in jail forever." She wiped a tear from her eye and smiled sheepishly. "My mascara's running, right? I probably look like the bride of Frankenstein."

"You look beautiful," Nancy said, laughing.

A middle-aged woman came up to Eileen and

offered her congratulations, so Nancy and George moved on. When they got through the receiving line, they proceeded to the ballroom, where the reception was taking place. A six-member blues band was playing a lively song, and several couples were already dancing.

"I'm going to check out front and see if Luke's here yet," George told Nancy. "See you later."

Nancy gave her a little wave, then reached down and smoothed the skirt of her green taffeta dress. A waiter came by with a tray of caviar canapés on heart-shaped pieces of toast. Nancy took one and popped it into her mouth. She stared out the window; snow was falling softly on the courtyard, dusting the trees and stone benches.

She felt a hand on her shoulder. "Jimmy got the string quartet for the ceremony, and Eileen got the Screaming Souls for the reception," a familiar voice murmured in her ear. "Figures, doesn't it?"

Nancy turned around. Noah was standing there, looking gorgeous as usual in a white vintage tux. "Hi, Noah. How have you been?"

"Fine, except for the mental and emotional anguish I suffered because you wouldn't be my date for this wedding," Noah complained.

"My boyfriend was supposed to be my date, but he had to go on a trip with his family," Nancy explained.

Noah grinned. "The boyfriend's not here? Great. That means you can dance every single dance with me."

Noah took her hand and started to pull her to the dance floor, but Nancy stopped him. "You know, there's something I've been meaning to ask you about what happened in August," she said. "Why did you lie about leaving your dad's party early?"

"You're still dredging up that ancient history?" Noah protested. He sighed when he saw the determined look in Nancy's eyes. "Oh, all right. The truth is, I had a fight with the old man at the party. I got so mad, I had to split. I'm sorry I left you guys there, but I wasn't thinking straight. I went to Sharkey's Pool Hall to work off some steam."

Nancy's curiosity was piqued. "What did you and your dad fight about?"

Noah shrugged. "Oh, the same old thing. He was giving me a hard time because I wouldn't get some brain-numbing job to support myself. He said he was tired of me bleeding my trust fund dry." He glanced disdainfully at his father, who was across the room. "His head is full of the weirdest ideas. I mean, what's money for if not to spend it, right?"

"So did you get your way? Has your dad stopped bugging you about getting a job?" Nancy asked him.

Noah frowned glumly. "Actually, no. You're looking at the new Fairfield, Inc., public relations assistant. I've been doing it for six weeks, and I'm already totally bored with it."

Then his face lit up. "I was kind of thinking of opening a restaurant, though. You know, call it Chez Noah or Noah's Bistro or Noah's Down-Home Cooking. I'm an awesome cook."

The Screaming Souls switched to a slow number. Noah put his hand on Nancy's arm. "Okay, now that you know I'm not a psycho freak criminal, will you dance with me? Come on, please?"

Nancy grinned. It was hard to resist Noah. "Okay, just one dance. Then I have some friends I want to catch up with."

Four dances later Nancy finally tore away from Noah and walked over to a table where the Hardys were sitting with Mr. Vaughn, Chelsea, George, and Luke.

"Hi, guys. Having fun?" Nancy called out.

Frank pulled out the chair next to him. "Get over here, Drew. I haven't had a chance to say hi to you yet—especially with that Fairfield guy totally monopolizing you."

Nancy sat down next to Frank and gave him a hug. She also hugged Joe, who was sitting on the other side of her. Then she said hi to the Vaughns and Luke.

"I was just telling the Hardy boys about Goldenrod," Mr. Vaughn said cheerfully to Nancy. The Texan was dressed in a tuxedo, red lizard boots, and a ten-gallon hat. "Except his new name is Chelsea's Prize. I bought him for my little girl here because she was so crazy about him."

"He's the best horse in the world, even though he isn't Golden Folly's real foal," Chelsea explained. She beamed at her father. "Daddy got him for me for my seventeenth birthday."

"Who did you buy him from, Mr. Vaughn?" Nancy asked. "Isn't Abe Addison in jail?"

"His wife sold Chelsea's Prize to me—and for way less than two million dollars," Mr. Vaughn replied. He sat back in his chair, stuffed an unlit cigar into his mouth, and smiled contentedly. "With all the money I saved on that deal, I bought myself a condo here in town. Chelsea and I are going to be visiting here more often. Nice little town, Saratoga."

Joe's eyes lit up. "That's awesome news," he told Chelsea. "You'll have to come to Bayport sometime while you're up here. It's not too far."

Chelsea nodded eagerly. "We can go riding together. How many horses does your family own?"

Frank chuckled, wondering how Joe was going to answer that one. Then he leaned toward Nancy. "I don't know if I told you, but we got a letter from Prince Zafir," he told her quietly.

"He said that the people who hired Berthe Lindgren have been caught and put in jail. He also thanked us for saving his life and told us we could visit him in Morocco anytime as guests of the palace." He added, "What do you think, Drew? Think you might want to go to Morocco with us some time?"

Nancy's eyes lit up. "Wouldn't that be great? The three of us in Morocco?"

Just then Jimmy and Eileen came by. "There you are, Nancy and George," Jimmy called out. "Just the people we wanted to see."

Eileen leaned over and grinned. "Jimmy has a little present for you two."

"A present?" George repeated, surprised. "What for? We didn't do anything."

"Oh, yeah, right," Jimmy said. "You only rescued me from a couple of kidnappers and a blazing fire. If it hadn't been for the two of you, this day wouldn't have been possible." He reached into the pocket of his tuxedo and handed Nancy and George two small boxes wrapped in white tissue paper.

Nancy and George opened them. Inside each was a silver necklace: a horse charm dangling from a long, delicate chain.

"It's beautiful," Nancy said, holding the necklace up to the light.

"Totally," George agreed.

"I hope they'll remind you of Saratoga,"

Jimmy said. "And I hope you'll both visit again next August. You can stay in the house Eileen and I just bought. And this time I promise, no more mysteries."

"Then what will Nancy do?" Joe said innocently.

Everyone burst out laughing.

FEAR STREET® SAGA

Collector's Edition

Including
The Betrayal
The Secret
The Burning

R·L·STINE

Why do so many terrifying things happen on Fear
Street? Discover the answer in this special
collector's edition of the *Fear Street Saga* trilogy,
something no Fear Street fan should be without.

Special bonus: the Fear Street family tree,
featuring all those who lived—and died—under the
curse of the Fears.

Available From Archway Paperbacks
Published by Pocket Books

POCKET
BOOKS

1233-01

FEAR STREET®

R.L. Stine

- ☐ THE NEW GIRL ....74649-9/$3.99
- ☐ THE SURPRISE PARTY ....73561-6/$3.99
- ☐ THE OVERNIGHT ....74650-2/$3.99
- ☐ MISSING ....69410-3/$3.99
- ☐ THE WRONG NUMBER .....69411-1/$3.99
- ☐ THE SLEEPWALKER ....74652-9/$3.99
- ☐ HAUNTED ....74651-0/$3.99
- ☐ HALLOWEEN PARTY ....70243-2/$3.99
- ☐ THE STEPSISTER ....70244-0/$3.99
- ☐ SKI WEEKEND ....72480-0/$3.99
- ☐ THE FIRE GAME ....72481-9/$3.99
- ☐ THE THRILL CLUB ....78581-8/$3.99
- ☐ SECRET ADMIRER ....89429-3/$3.99
- ☐ THE SECRET BEDROOM ..72483-5/$3.99
- ☐ THE KNIFE ....72484-3/$3.99
- ☐ FEAR STREET SAGAS COLLECTOR'S
  EDITION ....00298-8/$6.99

- ☐ THE PROM QUEEN ....72485-1/$3.99
- ☐ FIRST DATE ....73865-8/$3.99
- ☐ THE BEST FRIEND ....73866-6/$3.99
- ☐ THE CHEATER ....73867-4/$3.99
- ☐ SUNBURN ....73868-2/$3.99
- ☐ THE NEW BOY ....73869-0/$3.99
- ☐ THE DARE ....73870-4/$3.99
- ☐ BAD DREAMS ....78569-9/$3.99
- ☐ DOUBLE DATE ....78570-2/$3.99
- ☐ ONE EVIL SUMMER ....78595-6/$3.99
- ☐ THE MIND READER ....78600-8/$3.99
- ☐ WRONG NUMBER 2 ....78607-5/$3.99
- ☐ DEAD END ....86837-3/$3.99
- ☐ FINAL GRADE ....86838-1/$3.99
- ☐ SWITCHED ....86839-X/$3.99
- ☐ COLLEGE WEEKEND ....86840-3/$3.99
- ☐ THE STEPSISTER 2 ....89426-9/$3.99
- ☐ WHAT HOLLY HEARD ....89427-7/$3.99
- ☐ THE PERFECT DATE ....89430-7/$3.99
- ☐ NIGHT GAMES ....52958-7/$3.99

CATALUNA CHRONICLES

- ☐ THE EVIL MOON ....89433-1/$3.99
- ☐ THE DARK SECRET ..89434-X/$3.99
- ☐ THE DEADLY FIRE ...89435-8/$3.99

FEAR STREET SAGAS

- ☐ A NEW FEAR 52952-8/$3.99
- ☐ HOUSE OF WHISPERS
  52953-6/$3.99

SUPER CHILLER

- ☐ PARTY SUMMER ....72920-9/$3.99
- ☐ BROKEN HEARTS ....78609-1/$3.99
- ☐ THE DEAD LIFEGUARD ......86834-9/$3.99

FEAR PARK

- ☐ #1: THE FIRST SCREAM ....52955-2/$3.99
- ☐ #2: THE LOUDEST SCREAM ....52956-0/$3.99
- ☐ #3: THE LAST SCREAM ....52957-9/$3.99

Simon & Schuster Mail Order
200 Old Tappan Rd., Old Tappan, N.J. 07675

Please send me the books I have checked above. I am enclosing $_____ (please add $0.75 to cover the postage and handling for each order. Please add appropriate sales tax). Send check or money order—no cash or C.O.D.'s please. Allow up to six weeks for delivery. For purchase over $10.00 you may use VISA: card number, expiration date and customer signature must be included.

Name _____

Address _____

City _____ State/Zip _____

VISA Card # _____ Exp.Date _____

Signature _____

739-33

It's a new school year! And it's time for Fear!

Presents The

1997 Calendar

A sixteen month calendar that starts in
September. When your new year really begins!
It's a year and a half of horror! Your favorite Fear
Street guys and ghouls are back to send you
screaming through the school year with sixteen
months of ghostly, gruesome fun!

Plus a special bonus ... A poster of every
single Fear Street cover ever made! But be
careful—all together they may be more fear
than you can handle!

Available
from Archway Paperbacks
Published by Pocket Books

1249-01